Midnight Star

By

Ellen Dugan

Midnight Star

Cover art by Dar Albert
Daughters Of Midnight logo by Dar Albert
Editing by Katherine Pace
Copy Editing and Formatting by Libris in CAPS

Published by Ellen Dugan

ACKKNOWLEDGMENTS

As always, thanks to my family, friends, beta readers, and editors.

For Lyn and John for listening to me as I figured out there would indeed be a second trilogy in the Daughters Of Midnight series...

Special thanks to my honorary daughter Amber, and to her husband Armando Flores—and to both of his fabulous mothers: Sonia and Yvette. *Muchas gracias* for the cheerful answers to my many questions on common Hispanic slang, phrases...and swearing!

Other titles by Ellen Dugan

THE LEGACY OF MAGICK SERIES

Legacy Of Magick, Book 1

Secret Of The Rose, Book 2

Message Of The Crow, Book 3

Beneath An Ivy Moon, Book 4

Under The Holly Moon, Book 5

The Hidden Legacy, Book 6

Spells Of The Heart, Book 7

Sugarplums, Spells & Silver Bells, Book 8

Magick & Magnolias, Book 9

Mistletoe & Ivy, Book 10 (Coming 2019)

THE GYPSY CHRONICLES

Gypsy At Heart, Book 1

Gypsy Spirit, Book 2

DAUGHTERS OF MIDNIGHT SERIES

Midnight Gardens, Book 1

Midnight Masquerade, Book 2

Midnight Prophecy, Book 3

Midnight Star, Book 4

Midnight Secrets, Book 5 (Coming Soon)

The Four Stars Prophecy

There are four stars of magick that shine from a Midnight sky,

While three have been together, one was hidden from their sight.

Though the search was in vain, love will always find a way,

This fact will be made known to her on the saddest of days.

From the farthest western lands, the star must journey home,

To claim her place, no longer to wander...lost and alone.

-Ellen Dugan

Midnight Star

Be glad of life because it gives you the chance to love,

to work, to play, and to look up at the stars.

-Henry Van Dyke

PROLOGUE

It was official. This was the absolute *worst* birthday in the history of birthdays.

I managed to unlock my apartment door one-handed. Nudging the door open with my elbow I stepped inside, reached back, and bolted the door shut behind me. Shrugging the purse off my shoulder, I let it fall to the couch and carried the pizza box to the high kitchen counter.

I dropped the cardboard box, and it made a greasy sort of slap as it hit the counter. "You'll find another job, Estella," I said, simply for the comfort of hearing another voice. "A job where your boss isn't always trying to grab your ass."

It had been a horrible last few days. First, my old car had broken down and I had to start walking to work. Then my boss had decided his sleazy comments and innuendos weren't enough to successfully talk me into bed, so he'd groped me when I'd been working behind the bar.

My response to his ass-grab had been swift and violent. And the next thing I knew, I'd been fired. Not that I would have wanted to stay there after that anyway...but hell. Now I was unemployed, without a car, and damn-near broke.

I'd walked slowly home, down the dusty and dry streets of Bakersfield. I had barely enough cash left in my pocket to buy the pizza. With a sigh, I flipped the top of the pizza box open and took a look at my birthday dinner.

It was, as celebratory dinners go, fairly pathetic.

Resolutely, I squared my shoulders, marched to the fridge and took out my last beer. "Getting fired when I was already behind on the rent was pretty shitty timing," I muttered, and popped the top off the beer. "I'll figure something out. I've been in worse scrapes."

Although at the moment, I really couldn't recall things ever being this grim.

Glancing around, I wondered how much longer I would even be able to continue to live here. My studio apartment wasn't much to look at. My furniture consisted of items I'd purchased second-hand, or had rescued from a dumpster. The A/C kicked on and the airflow was stingy at best. I stepped over to my box fan and cranked it on high in the hopes that it would help cool things off.

The scent of the sausage pizza didn't quite mask the stale air in the apartment. I rooted around in a junk drawer, found a lighter, and lit the dollar store candle I had in the kitchen. After a moment, the scent of cinnamon drifted out and I set it beside the pizza box.

Resting my elbows on the counter and my chin in my hands, I sighed. "The only way to go is *up*," I reminded myself. Refusing to give in to defeat, I grabbed the small jar candle and decided it would have to do as a birthday candle.

My father had always said birthday wishes were magick...It was the one thing I could recall vividly about the man.

I held the jar candle at eye level and took a

deep breath. "Here's hoping," I said, shutting my eyes.

I wish that I wasn't always alone, I thought. *I wish I had a family and people who loved me.*

Then, I blew out the candle.

I opened my eyes and watched the smoke from the candle hover in the air for a moment and slowly dissipate. "Happy birthday to me." I picked up a piece of pizza and lifted it to my lips. Before I could take a bite, there was a knock on the door.

I sincerely hoped it wasn't the landlord coming to collect the rent. Silently, I moved to the door and checked the spy hole. It wasn't the landlord. Instead, a middle-aged man of average height and weight stood outside my door. My first instinct said *cop*, but I looked again, and wondered if he was a lawyer.

"Yes?" I called without opening the door.

"I'm looking for Estella Flores."

I took a deep breath and told myself that whatever happened next, I could handle it. I opened the door. "Can I help you?"

The man studied me cautiously. "You're Estella Flores?"

I gave the man in the suit the once-over. "Who wants to know?" I asked.

"My name is Todd Watson, I'm a private investigator."

Damn, that was fast, I thought. It had maybe been two hours since I'd broken that bottle of whiskey over the head of my *pendejo* of a boss. "Diego shouldn't have grabbed my ass," I said, planting my hands on my hips. "You go and tell him, that if he thinks he's going to press charges against me for assault—that I'll press charges against *him* for sexual harassment!"

The man blinked at me. "Excuse me?"

"Aren't you here because of what happened at the bar today?"

The man shook his head. "No. I'm not here because of that."

"What do you want?"

"Are you the daughter of Isabel Flores and Daniel Midnight?"

Midnight. That was a name I hadn't heard since I was small.

"Yes." I folded my arms over my chest. "What's this about?"

"Ms. Flores, your family hired me—"

"I don't have a family." I cut him off. "Both of my parents are dead and I'm an only child."

"Actually," he said, taking a card out of a folder. "That's not true. You do have a family. Your paternal grandmother, Priscilla Midnight, hired me to find you."

"Grandmother?" My jaw hit the floor. "I have a grandmother?"

Mr. Watson nodded and handed me his business card. "Yes, you do."

"I had no idea..."

"You look remarkably similar to your father," he said.

"How would you know?" I demanded.

He opened his folder back up and pulled out an old photo. "Because of this," he said, passing me a picture of my father and my mother that I'd never seen before. They were seated together, my father had his arm around my mother's shoulders. There was a toddler with dark brown pigtails sitting between them.

That toddler was me.

My breath whooshed out. "Where did you get this?"

"Your father sent it to your grandmother

twenty-two years ago."

"Holy shit." My hands started to tremble. "I never knew my father had any living relatives." I passed the picture back.

"Perhaps I could come in and we could discuss the matter in more detail?" He peered past me and inside my apartment as he spoke. "Or would you be more comfortable going somewhere public to speak to me?"

He was an honest man: I sensed that immediately. But still, I wasn't going to invite a stranger in to my apartment. "We can go out," I said. "Give me a couple of minutes to change out of my work clothes."

He stepped back. "There's a coffee shop on the corner. Why don't you meet me there...Let's say in five minutes?"

"Okay." I nodded. "Five minutes."

Mr. Watson smiled politely and left.

I closed the door, grabbed the pizza and stuck it in the fridge. I stripped off the bar uniform t-shirt, left my jeans and sneakers as they were, and grabbed a clean cotton blouse that had been drying in the bathroom. Pulling down my hair from the high ponytail I'd worn to work, I quickly brushed out my long hair.

I checked my reflection in the bathroom mirror while I buttoned up the black shirt. “This is crazy,” I said to my reflection. “I can’t believe this.”

The woman who regarded me seemed to agree. “It might be crazy,” I decided, dusting some powder over my nose. “But he had that picture. I’d be a fool not to find out if it’s true that I have a grandmother.” I pulled the star pendant I habitually wore out from my collar and laid it on top of my blouse.

I was out the door and walking down to the coffee shop in under three minutes flat. I turned the corner and, using the big potted blooming plant for cover, I leaned forward and checked through the window. There he was, sitting inside at a booth, looking at a menu.

As I stood there psyching myself up, a thin branch of neon-pink bougainvillea fell off the lattice where it had been climbing and was caught in my hair. I carefully freed myself from the thorny tendril and took a moment to tuck it back on the lattice. “There you go,” I said to the plant, and reached for the coffee shop’s door.

Mr. Watson waved me over as soon as I entered. "Would you like to order anything?" He smiled as I took a seat across from him. "I thought maybe I'd get a sandwich for dinner."

Shit, I thought. *I didn't have any cash on me. I'd spent the last of my money on that pizza.* I cleared my throat. "Just a water, please."

The waitress appeared. Mr. Watson glanced over at her. "We'll have two orders of your daily special," he said.

The waitress scribbled in her book. "Two orders of the vegetable soup and the turkey club. Anything to drink?"

"Two waters, please," Mr. Watson said. "And bring the check to me."

"Yes, sir." The waitress nodded and left.

"*Gracias*," I said.

Mr. Watson wasted no time getting down to business. The paperwork he had on my life was impressive. Copies of my birth certificate, drivers license, both of my parent's death certificates...it was a little intimidating. He even knew about my juvenile record.

"I was only fifteen." Unembarrassed, I smirked at the man. "I took a joyride in a friend's car...how was I supposed to know it had been stolen?"

He grinned. "You've lived a colorful life, Estella."

The man wasn't judging and his smile made me relax. "So," I said, "tell me about my grandmother."

Our food arrived and I dug in, listening as he filled me in on Priscilla Midnight. She lived in a farmhouse in Ames Crossing, Illinois—wherever the hell that was. The property had been passed down through her husband's family, and it was the farmhouse where my father had grown up.

"I never knew my father was born and raised in Illinois on a farm," I said. *Note to self,* I thought. *Do some internet digging on Illinois.*

"You weren't even five years old when he passed away, so that's not surprising. Didn't your mother tell you about him or his family?"

"After he died in action, my mother rarely spoke about him. When I got older and asked, she'd always say that it was too painful to discuss."

"I checked into your mother's life as well.

She was raised in the foster care system, and went directly into the military after she graduated high school."

I dabbed at my lips with a napkin. "I'm still trying to wrap my mind around the fact that I have a living relative. A grandmother, that actually wants to meet me."

Mr. Watson nodded. "She truly does. But you do have more than *one* relative."

My jaw dropped. "I do?"

"Ms. Flores you have three sisters, as well."

"Shut. Up!" I said.

"Daniel Midnight had three daughters from his first marriage. After your father died, his first wife surrendered custody of the girls to their paternal grandparents, who then raised them. After Priscilla's husband passed away, she continued to raise the three girls on her own."

"I wonder why their mother gave up custody?" I asked, despite myself.

"From what I've been told she wasn't very maternal, and she was upset that your father's death benefits had gone to his new wife and their child."

"Instead of her."

"Correct. Your half-sisters were never aware that their father had remarried—or that he'd had another child."

"So how do they feel about all of this?"

"To my knowledge your grandmother hasn't told them yet. She's tried unsuccessfully several times over the years to locate you. You haven't been easy to find."

"I'm betting my mother's career in the Air Force and our constant moving around didn't help."

"With your mother keeping her maiden name, and you going by Flores, it did make the search more challenging." Mr. Watson smiled. "But then Mrs. Midnight hired me. I've only been on the case for the past few months."

"So you're good at your job."

"I specialize in reuniting birth parents with the children they've given up for adoption—"

"Or adoptees trying to find their birth parents?" I guessed.

"Exactly." Mr. Watson rested his arms on the tabletop and leaned forward. "First, Priscilla wanted to locate you, and if you are amenable, for you to meet the rest of your family. I don't think she wanted to get your sisters' hopes up only to disappoint them if..."

"Sure, I get it." I nodded. "Does my grandmother know that you've found me?"

"She does, I've been in contact with her already." He reached across the table and rested his hand on mine. "Would you like to speak to her now?" His voice was kind.

I jolted a bit. "Ah, okay," was all I managed.

Mr. Watson gave my hand an encouraging pat. The he pulled a fancy cell phone from his pocket and punched in a number. "Hello, Priscilla," he said into his cell. "Yes, it's Todd. I have Estella here, she'd like to say hello." With a smile, he hit the speaker button and held the phone out toward me.

My mouth went bone dry as I leaned toward the phone. "Hello?"

"Estella?" The woman said. "Is that you?"

"Yes?" My hands were shaking. I tucked them out of view and in my lap.

"I've been looking for you for a *very* long time," she said.

"That's what Mr. Watson tells me," I

managed. "I'm sorry. I didn't know that I had a grandmother, or any other living relatives."

"Well, you most certainly do," she said firmly. "You are *not* alone, my dear. You are a daughter of Midnight, and your sisters will be so excited to meet you!"

I felt tears well up at her words, and I fought them back. "Thank you for searching for me."

"You're very welcome," she said, chuckling. "And by the way, happy birthday, Estella."

"Thanks," I said with a shaking voice. "It's been one for the books."

CHAPTER ONE

I'd been traveling for a solid day and a half, and now I was on the final leg of my journey. My flight to St. Louis was almost at an end. The plane descended through the clouds and I looked out the window, wondering what I'd see below. As the clouds thinned, a gasp escaped me. There were so many trees, and fields, and even more trees. I saw a river snaking back and forth, and everything was so incredibly *green*. After living in the high desert for the past five years, the Midwestern landscape below seemed very lush and almost alien to me.

In a matter of days, my entire life had completely changed, and my birthday wish had come true. Which I had to admit...was sort of spooky.

Bottom line? I had a family.

Besides my father's mother, I'd learned that I had three half-sisters as well: Drusilla, Gabriella and Camilla. I'd found out their names while speaking to my grandmother. I hadn't known what to expect from her, but I was touched by the genuine emotion in her voice. When she invited me to come to Ames Crossing, I grabbed ahold of the opportunity with both hands.

I knew sincerity when I heard it.

Call it a curse, or a superpower, but I instinctively know when folks are lying to me... and Priscilla Midnight hadn't been. She truly wanted me to come and stay with her. Mr. Watson had hand delivered an airline voucher to me the day after our initial meeting, and I'd left town later that night.

Which was no hardship. There was nothing left for me in Bakersfield. I sold my car for scrap and gave my furniture to the guy across the hall. I cleared out my scrawny excuse for a bank account, packed up what clothes I had, and got the hell out before my old boss, or the landlord, came looking for me. I'd deal with the issue of back rent later.

I'd caught a bus out the night I'd received the airline voucher and headed to LAX. It had been a long bus ride, but it had also given me plenty of time to think. I booked the first available flight the next morning, found a cheap hotel room close to the airport, and took advantage of the free Wi-Fi.

While Mr. Watson had told me about my relatives at our first meeting, the rest I'd found out by doing a dive into social media with my cell phone. The oldest, Drusilla, was a children's book author, a fairly well known one too. I checked her website and saw a number of pretty books about faeries and gardens. Her author photo was professionally done, very soft and romantic. With her long blonde hair, and a pretty face framed by bangs, Drusilla looked exactly how I'd imagined someone who wrote about faeries would.

Gabriella, the middle sister, was a graphic designer. Her black and white profile photo was more casual. Her hair was pale enough in the picture that I figured she too was a blonde. Turns out sister number two designed websites and romance novel covers. I checked out her website as well and smiled over the sexy cover art she'd designed. *Good for her,* I thought. Priscilla had told me that Gabriella—or Ella as she was called—was recently married and a new mother to boot.

The youngest of my half-sisters was Camilla. She ran a funky boutique called *Camilla's Lotions & Potions* in their hometown. With interest, I checked out her shop's website. There'd been a photo of her standing hip-shot behind the counter, and the pose had made me like her immediately. She seemed a bit rock and roll with her edgy pink hair and pierced nose.

After viewing the photos of each of my sisters, I didn't see much resemblance between us. For starters, they were blondes—like our father had been. Or two of them were blondes, I corrected myself. From what I could tell they all appeared to have blue or green eyes.

Being brown-eyed and brunette, I was going to stick out like a sore thumb next to my blonde sisters. With that thought in mind, I reached for my purse and pulled out the photo Mr. Watson had given me of myself with my parents.

I supposed that I did favor my father. The shape of my face, jaw line, and wavy hair were definitely from him. My coloring, however, was not. My mother's Hispanic heritage had seen to that. My hair was a deep brown, a shade or two lighter than my mother's black hair had been, yet my complexion was closer to my mother's. However, while she'd been petite, I was average height with a curvier frame.

I wondered how the news of my existence had gone over. Priscilla had stated that she'd be telling my sisters about me immediately...and I bet that had been a hell of a conversation. I imagined finding out they had a Latina half-sister hadn't gone over well. I didn't expect my father's other daughters to be all welcoming or loving, despite what Priscilla had said. Honestly? I expected the three of them would close ranks.

The announcement was made that we'd be landing shortly. I put my seat back up and told myself that I should look at this like a great adventure. It was crazy and ballsy moving across the country to live with relatives I'd never met. But anything had to be better than where I'd come from.

I tucked the photo away in my purse and picked up the heavy goldstone pendant from around my neck. I slid the star-shaped glass back and forth on its chain and tried to stay calm. The manmade blue glass was flecked with copper and it sparkled, like stars against a midnight sky...

Midnight. Priscilla had called me a 'daughter of Midnight', and I guessed that I was. It had been easier going by Flores in Bakersfield, as the name allowed me to fit in with other Latinos. But in Illinois, I wasn't sure that I would fit in. I'd researched Ames Crossing online as well last night, scrutinizing the photos of the quaint, historic riverside town. The sleepy village had looked like something out of an enchanted storybook.

Thinking about it all had me clutching for a moment. There was absolutely nothing quaint, quiet or charming about me. I'd never be described as a lady, or classy. I had a hell of a temper and knew how to use my fists when necessary. I was a fighter and a survivor. I'd had to be.

I raised my chin. *Be brave. Think of it like an adventure...* I told myself. This was a once in a lifetime chance to change my...well...to change my entire life. A determined woman could write her own damn destiny with a fresh start.

"Shoot for the moon and land in the stars," I whispered to myself as the wheels on the plane touched down.

***

I knew they were waiting for me.

I'd barely turned my cell phone back on after landing when I'd received a text from Priscilla Midnight. I had sent her a brief text message the night before with my flight number and ETA…and I supposed that my grandmother had texted me while I was mid-flight. She'd responded that she would be waiting for me outside of security—with a sign.

With some concern I read a second, new text message: *Welcome Home! We're waiting for you!*

"Oh shit," I mumbled, tucking my phone away and slipping my purse over my shoulder.

"We?" I'd hoped it would simply be Priscilla picking me up, but apparently that was not the way it was going to be.

I shuffled my way off the plane, hauling my purse and duffle bag, and ducked into a restroom. I took care of business, washed my hands, and combed my hair. My makeup was holding up, and I took an extra moment to swipe some balm over my dry lips. I straightened the collar of my denim jacket and checked my reflection.

My eyes were too big. I was pale from nerves, and looked much younger than I actually was. *Maybe I could use that to my advantage, now,* I thought. *I'd done it before, sometimes for sympathy, and sometimes to throw an opponent off guard…*

Slowly, I straightened my shoulders. There was no real reason to be so defensive. "You can handle yourself," I told my reflection, "and any situation you're thrown into." With a pounding heart I took a deep breath, picked up my bag, and started walking toward the exit.

I spotted them well before they saw me. The three women were standing together. Priscilla was tall, and her ash-blonde hair swung to her shoulders. She was striking for an elderly woman. She wore slacks and a bright plaid blouse. The other woman had a softer look about her. It was Drusilla, the oldest of the sisters. She stood wearing a casual dress and scanning the crowd. The third of the trio had to be Camilla—the pink hair was a dead giveaway. She wore knee-high boots over jeans and a pink leather jacket. She also held up a big sign with blue balloons attached to it. The sign read: "Welcome Home Estella!"

I walked along with the crowd and my palms were sweaty. My heart was pounding in my ears as I went down the short glass hall and cleared the security area. I watched as Priscilla's face lit up.

"Estella!" She rushed forward and I found myself grabbed up in an exuberant hug.

My duffle swung around and hit my back. Awkwardly, I gave her a pat on the shoulder with one hand. "Hello, Priscilla."

She stepped back holding me at arms length. "You look so much like your father."

And nothing like the rest of you, I thought.

I tried for a smile as Priscilla wiped tears from her eyes.

"Hi, I'm Dru." The woman in the dress stuck out her hand.

I clasped it. "Hello. Nice to meet you." I nodded to Camilla. "And you're Camilla?"

"Guilty," she said with a wink. "And I'm sure as hell not shaking your hand. It's not every day you find out you have a little sister. Come here, you!" She shoved the poster at Dru and grabbed me in a fierce hug.

Her enthusiasm had me smiling. "I dig your hair," I said when she let me go. "And the nose ring." I hitched the duffle bag up over my shoulder again.

Camilla grinned. "Holy cats! You're gorgeous, aren't you?" She gave me the once over, but it was friendly. "I'd kill for hair that color, and your eyes are like dark chocolate." She linked her arm in mine and steered me toward the baggage claim.

Dru tucked the sign under her arm. "Gabriella is at home with the baby and she's dying to meet you, Estella."

I nodded. "Okay," seemed like the safest

answer. I didn't even know the baby's name, gender, or how old it was.

Priscilla fell in step with us. "Let's go get your bags."

I tipped my head toward the duffle. "This is it," I said. "I'm good to go."

Priscilla paused for a moment, but took my other arm and I found myself being led outside to the short-term parking lot. The women chattered away as we walked to a dark blue SUV.

Dru hit her key fob and the locks popped. She put the sign in the back and reached for the duffle. "Let me stow this for you."

"*Gracias*—Thanks." I surrendered the duffle and Dru tucked it away.

"Sit up front," Dru invited me, and I walked around to the passenger side and climbed in.

Camilla and Priscilla let themselves in the back seat and I buckled myself in. "How far of a drive is it to Ames Crossing?" I asked.

"Not long," Dru said, sliding in the driver's seat. "Maybe thirty or forty minutes depending on the afternoon traffic."

I enjoyed the drive. It was interesting to see

the urban give way to the suburbs and then farm land. But I still couldn't get over how green it all was. Feeling slightly awkward, I chose a safe topic of conversation. "I thought maybe the trees would be turning colors already."

"Peak color is mid-October," Dru answered.

Up ahead I saw what appeared to be two gigantic sails. "What's that?"

"That's the Clark suspension bridge," Camilla said, pointing over my shoulder and out the front.

We crossed the first bridge even as the second, larger bridge grew closer.

"This is the Missouri River we're crossing," Dru said as she drove along. "This area is mostly wetlands and conservation areas."

"Wow, it's big," I said, looking out my window. As soon as we crossed the first bridge I could see yet another river, and that suspension bridge loomed closer still. "Good god." Both rivers were huge. I'd never seen any so wide.

"*Now* we're crossing the Mississippi river," Priscilla announced.

As we crossed the bridge I noticed a small state line sign, followed by a larger, *Welcome to Illinois.* We zipped through the old town of Alton, past a grouping of very tall, white silos and Dru turned left, following the river.

I tried to play it cool, but I couldn't help myself. I kept turning my head trying to take everything in as Dru explained about the great river road, the massive Mississippi river to my left and the trees and tall limestone cliffs to the right that were habitat for bald eagles. It was stunning.

"Eagle days are in January and February," Camilla piped up from the back seat. That's when we are flooded with tourists."

"And lots of folks come out to drive the river road to view the fall foliage as well," Priscilla pointed out.

"I had no idea that Illinois looked anything like this..." It was *primal* almost. There was something about it all that felt familiar too. I felt a shiver roll down my back. "This is amazing."

"Did you expect all flat farmland?" Camilla teased.

"Mr. Watson said you lived in a farmhouse, so I figured, you know, *farms*." My eyes scanned the trees that pushed right up to the base of the cliffs, and there were even more trees at the tops. I saw a brush of yellow and red in those green leaves, and it made me smile.

"We'll have to bring you back so you can see the Piasa bird another time," Dru said as she drove competently along the highway.

"What's a Piasa bird?" I asked.

"A local monster," Camilla said blithely from the back seat.

"Say what?" I twisted around to look at her.

She grinned. "Trust me. We have all sorts of monsters, ghosts and magick around here."

I didn't rise to the bait, but asked dozens of questions about the bluffs, trees and the river instead. As we neared the exit for Ames Crossing, Drusilla pulled off the highway and slowed down significantly as we drove through the village.

"Our farmhouse is outside of the village proper," Drusilla explained. She turned down a street and slowed to a stop in front of a brick house with a bump out on the top.

"What a cool old house." I opened the passenger window and leaned my head out to look.

"This is my fiancé's house," Dru explained.

"It's great," I said, admiring the fancy white woodwork trim on the second floor and sets of glossy black shutters. "What do you call the bump-out part on the top of the roof?"

"It's a cupola, and there's a widow's walk," Dru said. "I'll be moving in officially in a couple of weeks, after we get back from our honeymoon."

"Honeymoon?" I asked. "You're getting married soon?" Automatically I checked out her left hand. There was a pretty diamond and sapphire ring sparkling there, and a fancy manicure on her long fingers.

"In less than a week." Drusilla smiled. "Cammy is getting married this year as well. In December."

And I'd arrived and had probably thrown a giant wrench in the family's plans. "I'm sorry," I said immediately. "I wouldn't have come right away if I'd have known I'd be interrupting anything."

"Don't be ridiculous." Drusilla waved that away. "We're *thrilled* you could be here."

She meant it too, I realized. Her calm declaration had the nerves in my belly settling down. I nodded to Drusilla, and kept my mouth shut as Priscilla told me about the town. There was a variety of architectural styles and lots of quirky stone houses, compliments of the old Ames quarry, she explained. Apparently back in the day you could get a free parcel of land to build a house on *if* you got the stone to build the house from the local quarry.

"Here we are," Priscilla announced as we pulled down a long gravel drive. Ahead sat a pretty, two-story farmhouse. The house had a wide covered front porch and deep royal blue shutters against white siding. But what struck me most were the flowers. The house was surrounded by gardens. I'd never seen anything like it, unless it was from a glossy magazine.

"Welcome home." Priscilla rested her hand on my shoulder and gave it a squeeze.

I saw with some discomfort several people had spilled out of the front door and were standing waiting on the porch.

Oh boy, I thought. *Now it's time to meet the rest of the gang.* I counted seven more people. Three men, a woman with blonde wavy hair holding a baby, a little blonde boy, and finally an older girl with red hair.

So much for quietly settling in, I thought. I was about to run the gauntlet.

Dru parked the SUV and everyone piled out. I took a deep breath and was the last to exit the car. I looped my purse over my shoulder and found that Priscilla had moved up behind me.

"Don't be nervous," she said. "Everyone is excited to meet you." The arm she put around my shoulders was likely intended to be comforting, but I wondered if she'd done that so I wouldn't bolt.

When I'd tended bar, I'd faced down mean drunks, broken up bar fights, and on one memorable occasion was robbed at gunpoint. But this...this scared me more than anything else I'd ever experienced. *But I'd be damned if I'd let them know that.* I lifted my chin, tossed my hair over one shoulder and marched up to the porch steps.

"Everyone, this is Estella," Priscilla said,

easily.

I was introduced to Jacob and Jaime Ames—Camilla's fiancé and his son. The tall man with brown hair and intense blue-green eyes was Drusilla's fiancé, Garrett Rivers. The red-haired girl was his niece, Brooke.

Garrett shook my hand and welcomed me to the family, while the red-haired girl hovered at his side, giving me a suspicious look. She didn't say hello.

Lastly, I was introduced to my other sister, Gabriella and her husband Philippe.

She smiled and her eyes filled with tears. "Oh my god, you really look like our dad!"

"So I've been told." I tried to smile, but didn't quite pull it off.

"This is my daughter, Danielle" Gabriella gestured to the baby.

"*Ay, mi muñeca!*" I couldn't help but smile at the baby. She had a head of dark hair, like her father's, but blue eyes like her mother. "How old is she?" I asked.

"Six months," said Philippe. "Hello, Estella."

My brows rose at his French accent. "Hi."

Priscilla smoothly took over. "Well, let's get

you settled." She steered me inside and the family trooped along after us. The group quickly dispersed. I could smell that someone was cooking, and I checked the clock on the mantle. It was after 5pm, and it sounded like the family was about to put dinner on the table.

I glanced around at the pretty living room and saw a leather sofa, linen-colored walls, and a brick fireplace. The home's furnishings were rustic. But these weren't clever reproduction farmhouse pieces. This furniture was, for the most part, antiques. Lived in and well-tended antiques. Which was about as foreign to me as the lush green grass, pretty trees, flowers and that huge river.

I was shown upstairs, and Camilla insisted on hauling my duffle up for me. Priscilla opened the second door on the right and I found myself in a small bedroom. The walls were off white, and the floors were a gleaming hardwood. Under a window, a curvy old iron bed held a full-size mattress and was covered with a vintage white chenille bedspread. An antique red and white quilt was folded over the end of the bed, and plump pillows sewn from timeworn quilts, also in red and white, made it seem inviting. I spotted a nightstand, and a sturdy wooden dresser across the room. It was simple, but warm and welcoming. A padded bench sat at the end of the footboard and Camilla dropped my duffle on it.

"We thought you'd be comfortable here," Priscilla said.

"It's very pretty," I said around the lump in my throat. Actually, it was beautiful. I'd never stayed in such a nice room. I'd lived in Air Force base housing with my mother most of my life, serviceable but with no character whatsoever. After her death, I'd lived in whatever cheap apartment I could find.

"The bathroom is right across the hall," Camilla said. "We all share that."

I nodded. "Okay."

"My room is at the top of the hall on the right," Camilla said. "Dru's was the first door you passed."

"My bedroom is down on the main floor," Priscilla said, before I could ask. She smiled and rubbed a hand over my shoulder. "Why don't we give you a bit to settle in?"

“Thank you.” I nodded.

“Dinner is in a half hour,” Priscilla said. “Come downstairs when you’re ready.”

With a smile, the Midnight women left me on my own. I dropped down on the padded bench and looked around at the room in wonder.

I was here, and I hadn’t a god-damn clue what would happen next.

CHAPTER TWO

My first night in Illinois was spent staring at the ceiling and listening to the quiet. Or rather the crickets, frogs and cicadas that serenaded me through the open window. I didn't expect to sleep much, for I was too wound up and there'd been a lot of information to process and people to meet yesterday.

The family dinner hadn't been as awkward as I'd thought. I'd gone downstairs after tucking my clothes away in the old dresser and found myself sitting at the kitchen table and talking to Camilla and her fiancé Jacob.

Jacob ran a landscaping crew, currently lived in the village with his family, and his son Jaime was five. Jamie was a pistol and wanted to know if I'd ever been to Disneyland.

Drusilla had introduced me to Garrett, and I found out the gardens I'd admired were Drusilla's work. Priscilla and her husband had originally planted them, but it was Drusilla who'd taken on their refurbishment last year. Brooke—the redhead—was Garrett's ward, and she sat silently next to Dru and watched me like a hawk.

While my grandmother gave Gabriella a hand finishing dinner, I spoke briefly to Gabriella's husband, Philippe. He was sort of suave and sophisticated, but he didn't seem to be uptight about it. He bounced his daughter on his knee while the baby blew spit bubbles and cooed. When Gabriella had called to him to carve the roast, he'd passed the baby off to Drusilla, who'd tucked Danielle into a high chair.

The Midnights seemed to be going out of their way to make me feel at home. I listened to them talk about their lives and the winery that Garrett and Philippe owned, and of course Drusilla and Garrett's impending wedding.

When Drusilla asked me where I'd gone to school and what I did for a living, I was blunt and honest.

I'd never gone to college, and as to my career, best I could say was: waitress, bartender and for a memorable six months I'd worked security at a strip joint. That particular job had paid well, and no one ever expected that a woman would be the person keeping the patrons away from or out of the dancer's dressing rooms. I decided at the last second not to mention the *strip-club* part of my past—I didn't figure that would go down well with the roast beef.

I'd sat back and waited to see what the group reaction would be to my lack of college education, but there was no condescension, or worse, sympathy. Camilla wanted me to come into the village tomorrow and visit her shop, and I found that I was actually looking forward to it.

***

Stretching my arms over my head, I yawned. I snagged my phone from the nightstand and checked the time. It was 5:45 am and the sky was brightening in the east. I sat up and ran my fingers over the bright pink clusters of flowers that were trailing from a tiny vase on the nightstand. They were so pretty with their tiny white centers...I wondered what sort of flower they were? I'd never had anyone give me flowers before, and I found that I liked having them in my room, even this dainty vase of them. It was comforting somehow.

I got up, tossed my jeans on and shrugged a t-shirt over my head. A bit later, I headed down to the kitchen. I'd been told to make myself at home, so I padded barefoot in to the kitchen and headed for the fridge. After pouring myself a glass of juice, I decided that I wanted to take it outside on the back porch and watch the sun come up.

I shivered in the morning chill, and vaguely wished for a jacket, but wasn't uncomfortable enough to get up and go fetch mine. Sitting on the bottom step next to a large mixed container of flowers, I faced east and watched as the sun rose over the tree line. Enjoying the quiet, I slid my star pendant back and forth on its chain, while the birds hopped around the branches of the old tree in the back yard.

I leaned back on my elbows and sighed. *It was so peaceful here.* With some surprise, I saw a tortoiseshell cat come strutting across the backyard. It walked right up to me and meowed.

"*Buenos dias, gatito*," I greeted the cat who was now sniffing my bare toes.

"That's Mama Cat." Drusilla's voice from behind had me jerking in surprise.

"Morning, Drusilla," I said, as Drusilla came down the porch stairs.

"You can call me Dru," she invited and sat beside me on the bottom step. "Did you sleep well?"

"I didn't sleep," I said, eyeballing a much more casually dressed Drusilla. "Didn't expect to."

"Too wound up?" she asked, tugging an old ball cap over her head.

"Time change I guess." I shrugged. "I didn't figure anyone else would be awake."

"We're early risers around here." She pulled her blonde ponytail through the back of her cap. "I thought I'd get some work done in the gardens before breakfast."

Drusilla—Dru was wearing old jeans, beat up boots and a t-shirt that had seen better days. The complete change from the pretty dress she'd worn yesterday had me reconsidering her.

"You surprise me Dru," I said. "I figured a writer would be—"

"Sitting in my studio, sipping tea and listening to Enya?" Dru finished for me.

I snorted out a laugh. "Something like that."

"I enjoy gardening," she said. "It relaxes me."

I glanced over at her pretty manicure. "With your wedding so close I hope you have some gloves to protect that manicure with."

Dru pulled a pair out of her pocket. "Got it covered."

I reached out and patted Mama Cat who had started to rub against my ankles. "So are you nervous about the big day?" It seemed like the politest thing I could think to say to the woman—my sister.

Dru blew out a long breath. "I didn't expect I would be nervous about my wedding to Garrett, but I am." She smiled. "But it's the good kind.

A wound up and excited nervous."

I nodded. "This flower, here." I ran a finger over the cluster of red blossoms that trailed over the edge of the pot. "There's pink ones like this in a little vase in my room. What are they?"

"Those are red verbena. The flowers in your room are trailing pink verbena," Dru said.

"They're pretty."

"In the language of flowers, pink verbena signifies 'family unity'."

"No shit?" I tipped my head, considering what she'd said.

"No shit," she responded, straight faced. "Do you like flowers?"

"Sure," I said. "What's not to like?"

Dru smiled. "What's your favorite?"

"Bougainvillea," I said immediately.

"Passion and beauty." Dru nodded. "That would suit you."

Not sure what she meant, I shrugged. "I love the bright colors and how they climb all over everything."

"That's considered a tropical plant." Dru smiled. "I tried growing it in pots a few times, but it never gets very large here, and as soon as it gets cold—it dies."

"It grows huge in California."

"I'll bet." Dru stood and tugged her gloves on. "Come on, I'll give you a tour of the gardens."

"Okay." I scrambled up to follow her. The tortoiseshell cat stuck her tail in the air and followed along.

Dru walked me around the garden, pointing out the different plants. It was impressive the amount of knowledge she had.

"Wow, you know your plants," I said.

"I'm a daughter of Midnight. Herbalism and plant lore are a part of our heritage." She waited a beat. "It's your heritage too."

I wasn't sure how to answer that, so I remained silent.

"Why don't you give me a hand planting some daffodil bulbs?" Dru said.

I stuck my hands behind my back. "I don't know how to plant flowers."

"Well, it's high time that you learned." Dru took my arm in a tight grip and tugged me with her. "Trust me. It won't hurt a bit."

I shook my head. "*Jueges tanto!*"

"Did you swear at me?" Dru said, even as she kept right on hauling me along.

"No, I said that you are 'playing too much'."

"I knew I should have paid more attention to my high school Spanish classes," she muttered.

"If it makes you feel any better," I said. "I don't speak fluent Spanish. I just know some expressions—and lots of curse words."

"Do me a favor and don't teach the curse words to Brooke," Dru said. "She already swears in perfectly accented French, thanks to Philippe."

That thought had me laughing and I was cheerfully pulled toward a small rustic building in the back. The sign above the door announced it to be *Dru's Shed*. In no time at all I found myself next to Dru, kneeling in the grass along the edge of one of the flower beds and learning how to plant daffodils.

"Pointy end up?" I asked, holding up a bulb.

"That's right." Dru dug another hole. "Drop it in. Put three bulbs together in the hole."

I did as instructed, then patted the soil on top of the bulbs as Dru had shown me. "What color will these be?"

"These are white with yellow trumpets." Dru handed me the tag on the mesh bag of bulbs so I could see the photo of the flower. "They'll be pretty here in the shade gardens. The pale color will really stand out at night."

While I worked companionably with Drusilla in the backyard, the sun rose higher and the temperature grew warmer. We finished the task and Dru gathered up the hand spade and empty mesh bags.

"So now we wait for them to come up?" I asked, stretching out on the grass.

"You'll have a long wait," Dru said. "They won't bloom until late March."

"Why are you planting them now?"

"Because they need to winter over to bloom in the spring."

I looked around the garden. "I'm looking forward to watching the seasons change...You get snow here, right?"

"Oh, yeah," Dru said. "It's a safe bet you'll see plenty of snow living in Illinois."

"I suppose I'll have to get a winter coat," I said, mostly to myself.

"How long did you live in California?" Dru

asked.

"My mother was stationed at Edwards Air Force base for several years. After she died four years ago, I moved to Bakersfield, trying to get a job."

Dru frowned. "You've been on your own since you were twenty-one?"

"Um hmm," I answered distractedly. "Hey, Dru, what color does this tree turn?"

"That's a red oak," Dru explained. "It'll be a rusty brown, maybe red, depending on how the color is this year."

"'How the color is?' You mean it's not always the same?"

Dru walked over to stand next to me. "To get really spectacular color in the fall foliage we need cool nights and lots of sunny days."

I tipped my head back and studied the crown of the tree. "I didn't know that."

"I'll tell you what," Dru said. "I planned on making a run to the nursery today, to get some cornstalks and pumpkins to decorate for the autumn equinox—the fall season." Dru put her tools away in the shed and came back out. "Why don't you come with me? It will give you a chance to see more of the village."

I brushed the dirt from my hands. "Camilla mentioned that she wanted me to see her shop today."

Dru nodded. "We can swing by *Lotions & Potions* after we go to the nursery."

I climbed to my feet. "That could be fun."

"I knew I liked you." Dru grinned at me. "You like flowers and it sounds like you'd enjoy going plant shopping."

"I've never planted anything before." I said. "Thanks for teaching me. I enjoyed it."

"Girls!" Priscilla stood on the back porch waving us in. "Breakfast is ready!"

"Perfect!" Dru flashed a big smile and looped her arm through mine. "Let's go see what Gran conjured up for breakfast."

***

Drusilla, it ended up, was *not* as I'd imagined. Watching her competently pull weeds and dig in the dirt this morning had me re-evaluating her. She further blew my perception by taking the family's old pickup truck for a drive into town.

The truck she drove wasn't pretty. There were rust spots on the door and tailgate, but it ran well. I'd have never taken Drusilla Midnight as such a practical down-to-earth woman...her fancy author photo had completely fooled me. But I discovered that I could be comfortable in her company.

We tooled through the village with the windows down and I started to relax. It wasn't too tough of a job, to sit back and appreciate the breeze off the river. A short drive later, she pulled into the *River Road Garden Center.*

Hay bales were stacked attractively around the entrance. Cornstalks were on display and potted flowers in a rainbow of colors bloomed everywhere. "Chrysanthemums, right?" I asked as we walked along.

"Yup." Dru rubbed her hands together. "I promised Cammy I'd plant her some new window boxes outside her shop."

I trailed along behind Dru as she selected a flat of orange, purple and black flowers. I snuck a look at the plant tag. "Trick-or-treat, pansies?"

Dru tugged her cap down by the brim. "Yes. Pansies prefer the cooler temperatures. These will hold until November."

Dru ended up buying not only the pansies, but several bundles of cornstalks, two hay bales, a half dozen mums, and orange and white pumpkins in several different sizes. A nursery employee swung the hay bales in the back of the truck, but Dru loaded everything else herself.

Dru whipped the old truck back into the village and parked right in front of Camilla's shop. I spied the pretty display in the front window and hopped down from the truck to get a closer look.

A vintage white claw foot tub was featured. It was filled with sparkly clear cellophane and iridescent plastic spheres, giving the appearance of overflowing bubbles. A bath tray was centered over the tub and handmade soaps, and bottles of lotion were cleverly presented. Fluffy towels in pale pink and white were stacked around the tub, and on rustic wooden crates, more bath products were arranged. A white, chippy wooden sign announced the store was

Camilla's Lotions & Potions.

"Wow," I breathed.

"Pretty, isn't it?" Dru asked as she came around the hood of the truck. "Head on inside. I'll grab the pumpkins for Cammy."

I couldn't wait to see inside the boutique. I reached for the front door and let myself inside. Old bells jingled as the door opened and Camilla came out from the back, carrying an old wooden box. She was wearing a skater style dress that had moons and stars scattered all over it. Her practical flats were soundless on the hardwood floors. When she spotted me, Camilla smiled.

"Hey, Estella! What do you think?" she asked.

"This is awesome," I said, surveying the inside of the boutique.

Sturdy shelves lined the walls, and they were filled with a variety of items. With a quick scan, I spotted jars of lotions, bars of soap, and bottles of shampoo. In the center of the space, a large oblong rustic table held stacks of soaps, apothecary jars filled with more bath items, and there was even a vintage mortar and pestle.

"I got the pumpkins you wanted," Dru called as she let herself in behind me.

Camilla set the box on her check-out counter. "Set them on the center display table," she said.

"I can help," I said, and went to go carry in the rest of the pumpkins. Before I knew it, I was standing with Dru and Camilla and was being asked my thoughts on the fall display Camilla was currently building.

Dru adjusted a fat white pumpkin, while Camilla tucked moss around its base. "The white pumpkins are neutral enough, they don't clash with your product," she said.

"It's kind of early to decorate for Halloween, isn't it?" I asked. "Or do you get started earlier because of retail?"

"Oh, this is simply for the fall." Camilla grinned at me. "I'll go all out for Halloween."

While Dru went out to start planting up the boxes out front, Camilla showed me around and gave me a little demonstration on her products.

"You made all of this?" I asked.

"Sure." Camilla straightened a display of lip balm. "I've been open for almost nine months, and I've been working hard to stock up for the fall and future holiday sales."

I picked up an orange soap shaped like a leaf and gave it a sniff. "This smells amazing." I saw Drusilla out front sitting on the sidewalk and tucking pansies in the long window box under the store's front window.

Camilla dropped a hand on my shoulder. "Dru's happier planting the box by herself."

I jolted a bit. I'd just been wondering if I should go out and offer to help. "You a psychic or something?" I asked lightly.

"Or something." Camilla's lips curved up the tiniest bit.

"I like your shop," I said, and picked up a tester from the table. The label said it was rose and sandalwood lotion, and I squirted a dab on my fingers, lifted them to my nose, and sniffed. "Oh," I inhaled again. "I *love* this."

"Glad to hear it," Camilla said. "The lotions I make are all natural. That particular blend promotes healing, love and protection. The sandalwood is also highly spiritual."

"That's interesting," I said, adding some more lotion to the back of my hand. "Dru said something this morning about your family being into herbalism."

Camilla nodded. "Yes, we are. Actually, I was wondering..."

"Yes?" I said, rubbing the lotion in my hands.

"Would you like to help me out here at the shop on a part-time basis?"

I blinked. "Are you kidding?"

"Nope. I'll never be anything but honest with you." Camilla shook her head. "I have a feeling that truthfulness is very important to you."

I nodded. "It is."

Camilla nodded. "You said last night that you used to tend bar, so I'm sure you can more than handle any retail sales here."

"But you barely know me," I sputtered.

"I trust my instincts, and I was going to have to run an ad in the paper or put up a 'help wanted' sign. I can't do this all on my own during the fall and holidays, especially with my own wedding in three and a half months."

I thought over her offer. The truth was, I would need to get a job. It wasn't in my nature to live off someone else's charity. I'd figured I'd look around for a job tending bar in Alton, but I'd need a car for that. However, if I worked part-time with Camilla, it would give me a chance to save some money, pay off that back rent, and get to know the locals while keeping my eyes open for something full time.

"How about if we do this on a trial basis?" Camilla said. "You help me out for a couple of weeks and decide if you like it, and we'll see how it goes from there?"

"I don't know very much about the herbalism stuff." *But I could damn sure learn,* I decided as I looked around. *Note to self, Estella: Do some surfing on the web tonight and look up herbalism.*

"Knowing herbalism isn't a prerequisite to working here," Camilla said, tucking a lock of pink hair behind her ear. "Don't worry, I'll teach you."

I stuck my hand out. "This will be a huge step up from the last job I had, and god knows it smells a hell of a lot better." *And at least,* I mused as she shook my hand. *I wouldn't have to worry about getting my ass grabbed.*

"Great!" Camilla said. "And Estella...I promise not to grab your butt when you bend over in front of me."

I froze.

My half-sister stood there continuing to hold my hand. Her green eyes were direct and absolutely calm.

"You said you weren't psychic," I said, slowly.

"No. I actually said, 'or something' when you asked me if I was."

I studied her face. "Are you messing with me?"

"Not on purpose." Camilla raised one darkened brow. "You're not afraid, are you, Estella?"

"Of you?" I grinned at the challenge. "No, of course not."

"I like you." She gave my hand a friendly squeeze and then let go. "It'll be good for us to work together. This way we can get to know each other, and you'll have the chance to learn about the Midnight family's traditions."

"That, and I really need a job," I said, as she walked to her counter.

"Come on, let me show you around." She waved me over to join her at the check-out counter. “This is going to be so much fun.”

“I’ve never had a job that was fun.”

“Well that’s about to change.” She winked. “I’m going to teach you so much...you’ll never be bored here, Estella. I can promise you that.”

CHAPTER THREE

I went home from the shop with a book on herbs, and spent a few hours helping Dru decorate the front porch at the farmhouse. Which it ended up, was a lot of fun. I'd never decorated for the fall before. After we finished arranging the pumpkins and tying the cornstalks to the posts on the front porch of the farmhouse, I spent the rest of the afternoon thumbing through the herbal field guide book that Camilla had given me.

I managed to stay awake until about seven o'clock that evening. After forty-eight hours with no sleep, I face planted in that cozy bed. I managed to pull the quilt over myself before my body took over and put me down.

***

Thunder was rumbling and lightning flashed in the distance as a man held me close, kissing me passionately. He pressed kisses to my face and hair swearing that he loved me. He told me he'd do anything, if it meant we could finally be together...and that he couldn't live without me.

But his declaration didn't feel loving or romantic, because I was afraid. When he asked me to run away with him, I refused. It hurt me to do it, but I did. Terrified, I yanked away from him and then...I ran.

As fast and as far away as I could.

The storm broke, and the rain that fell mixed with my tears. I could barely see. My long skirts twisted around my legs and caused me to fall—hard. I pushed myself to my feet and continued on...even though my heart was breaking. All of my hopes and dreams were completely shattered, but I had to escape. I had to return home.

Still, he shouted after me.

Victoria, I love you!

His desperate voice woke me up.

I sat straight up, sweaty and disoriented. I felt around for the lamp on the nightstand and clicked it on. The soft light helped, and I dropped back against the pillows waiting for my heart rate to settle.

"What in the actual fuck?" I muttered. "That was crazy!"

I patted my galloping heart and struggled to recall what the man in the dream had looked like. He'd been young, with dark eyes and darker hair that brushed his shoulders. We'd been standing alone on cliffs that overlooked a valley. Behind us there'd been a huge old house...and the harder I tried to recall the features of the house, the less I could actually remember.

Checking my phone, I discovered it was 5:00 am. I'd been down for ten hours straight. Clearly I'd been more tired than I realized. I shoved the covers aside and rolled out of bed. "That's what I get for going without sleep for so long..." I scrubbed my hands through my hair and headed across the hall to the bathroom.

I'd throw myself head first into the shower and see if that helped snap me out of the crazy dreams. With one quick yank, I turned the water on and adjusted the shower spray to hot. I stripped, stepped right under the pounding spray, and tipped my face up to the water.

***

An hour later I sat at the kitchen table, trying to persuade Priscilla to let me help her with breakfast.

"Nonsense," she said, stirring the eggs in the skillet.

"Priscilla," I began.

"Gran," she corrected me. "You should call me Gran, like your sisters do."

I dodged that. I'd only known about the woman for a few days. It seemed a tad disrespectful to call her *Gran* so quickly. "Well let me make some toast, at least."

She nodded. "I'll allow that."

I got up and with her directions, located the bread, and stuck some slices in the toaster. I heard footsteps, and Camilla and Dru swung down the kitchen stairs.

"Gran is a little territorial with her new

stove," Camilla said. "Don't take it personally."

"*Que terca*," I muttered under my breath.

"What did you say to me, young lady?" Gran swung around. The spatula was raised, poised to swat at my butt, but there was a smile on her face.

"Oh, you've done it now!" Dru chuckled from across the kitchen. "Look out! Gran's got the spatula!"

"Save yourself!" Camilla laughed.

"*Nada*. I said nothing." I grinned and ducked out of the way.

Priscilla raised one arched brow. "It didn't sound like *nothing*."

"Oh, that's where Camilla gets the raising one eyebrow thing," I said. "From you."

"Humph," Priscilla sniffed.

"I only said that you were stubborn," I tried to mollify her.

"That better be all that you said." Priscilla narrowed her eyes. "Get the toast."

On cue the toast popped up. I slid my eyes from her face to the toaster.

That was weird.

Without a word, I grabbed the toast, put it on

a plate, and carried it to the table.

I'd barely taken my seat when Camilla leaned over and whispered. "She only threatens people she loves with the spatula."

"Oh yeah?"

"Or, if you swear at her in French." Dru sat across from me. "Just ask Brooke."

I bit the inside of my mouth to keep from laughing out loud. I found the mental image of the sullen, red-haired preteen getting whapped with a spatula immensely satisfying.

"I don't give a fig what language...English, French or Spanish," Gran said, setting a bowl of scrambled eggs on the table. "If you are disrespectful to me, I will retaliate."

"I'll keep that in mind," I said, straight-faced.

Priscilla passed me the bowl of eggs. "Are you headed in with Camilla this morning?"

"Umm hmm." I scooped up some eggs and passed the bowl. "I read some of that book you gave me, Camilla."

"That's good," she said, "and please, call me Cammy."

"I did recognize a few of the herbs in that formal herb garden out back," I said.

"Which plants were you able to identify?" Dru wanted to know.

"The purple coneflowers and rosemary," I said from around my eggs. "But your rosemary is so small here. It grows into shrub size in California. Oh, and the lavender, but I smelled it first...then I found it."

"We have a few different varieties of lavender in our gardens," Dru said. "Hidcote and Munstead."

"Okay." I nodded, making a mental note to look at them again.

"You have much to learn, my young apprentice," Cammy said in a passable Yoda impression. "We'll get into that more when we open the shop at ten."

I rolled my eyes at her silliness while Dru talked about her meeting with the wedding coordinator. She was doing an enchanted garden theme, which fit her. I knew because I'd seen the fancy wedding invitation that was stuck on the front of the fridge. Content, I let the conversation flow over me while I finished my breakfast.

"—and I can't believe the rehearsal diner is

tomorrow," she was saying. "It seemed like it was so far away and now...the wedding is in only two days."

"Do you have a dress to wear for the wedding, Estella?" Priscilla asked.

I didn't want to meet my grandmother's eyes. Truthfully, I didn't own a dress. I couldn't afford to buy one, and after listening to them all talk about the wedding, I knew it would be a formal event. Slowly, I set down my mug of tea. "I wasn't sure if I should go."

"What?" Drusilla's eyes were round. "Why wouldn't you?"

"You barely know me." I pointed out. "It's not a big deal, Dru."

"It *is* a big deal." Drusilla leaned her forearms against the table. "You are family, and I want you to be there."

"Well, I..." I trailed off when Priscilla rested a supportive hand on my arm. "The truth is," I said, before I changed my mind, "I don't own dressy clothes, and I can't afford to buy any right now. I wouldn't want to embarrass you by showing up in something inappropriate for your wedding."

"If you think I'm going to let you sit at home and be left out like some modern-day Cinderella," Dru said, firing up. "You've got another thing coming."

I grinned despite being embarrassed. "Dru, you are hardly a wicked step-sister."

"What size are you, Estella? An eight or ten?" Cammy asked.

"I don't know." I shrugged "I haven't worn a dress in years."

"Come with me. Upstairs," she said. "Let's go dive in my closet. You can borrow something of mine."

I looked her over. "I'm curvier than you are. Your clothes probably won't fit me."

Despite my protests, I was promptly herded up the stairs and into Camilla—Cammy's room. Dru and Priscilla came along too, and the next thing I knew, I was standing there in my bra and panties while my pink-haired sister started pulling things out of her closet.

I told myself to suck it up, and *not* to be embarrassed by standing in the middle of the room in my underwear with people I hardly knew.

Cammy waved a simple black dress. "Here, this will work."

I accepted the dress she shoved at me. "I don't think it will fit."

"It's stretchy," she argued. "It's a jersey type of fabric. Try it on anyway."

I pulled the short-sleeved dress over my head, tugged the hem down, and turned to look in the full-length mirror on the back of the door. To my surprise, the dress did fit. It was a tad snug in the bust, but otherwise, not too bad. It had a simple rounded neckline with a cinched in waist, and a hem that ended above my knees.

"Cute!" Dru said, coming around behind me to pluck and tug at the sleeves.

Automatically, I pulled my star pendant out and let it rest on the bodice of the dress. "I'm surprised it fit."

"You can't go wrong with an LBD. This is perfect for the rehearsal dinner." Dru said, smiling at me from over my shoulder.

I met her eyes in the mirror. "If you're happy with it, I am."

"Ah-ha!" Cammy cried, and pulled out a garment covered in a bag from the depths of her closet. "Here it is." She pulled the plastic off the dress hanger. "I bought this dress online last year, for New Years Eve, but it didn't fit me. So I've never worn it."

I eyeballed the sequined navy-blue dress. "I don't know..."

Cammy shoved the dress at me. "It was too loose on me, but with your bust line I bet it will be smokin' hot on you."

"Well, I—"

"Take the black dress off, and try the blue one on now," Dru said, cutting off my excuse without mercy.

"*Dios mio*!" I started to laugh at her bossy tone of voice.

Priscilla spoke up from the vanity stool where she'd sat to oversee the fashion show. "Think of it as a bonding experience with your sisters, dear."

I rolled my eyes at the lot of them, but I tried on the sequined dress. "Wow," I managed when I checked my reflection.

Cammy was right. It was smokin' hot.

The dress fit as if it were made for me. The dress was also a stretchy polyester type of fabric and it was covered in shinning navy-blue sequins. It featured a scooped neckline and three-quarter sleeves.

"That style totally works on you," Cammy said as she stood next to me studying my reflection.

The dress hit me mid-thigh. "Is it too short?" I asked them.

"I think it's perfect!" Dru bounced up and down.

"I'll need to borrow some shoes," I told her.

"No worries," Dru said. "I'm sure that between the two of us we have some black heels you can borrow."

"*Gracias*," I said to my sisters. "The dresses are very pretty, and I'm pleased to wear them."

"Hooray!" Cammy gave a fist pump. "That wedding crisis has been averted. Let's get this all put away and then me and you, Estella, we need to get ready to open the shop."

***

My first day at the shop passed quickly. Camilla—Cammy taught me how to ring up the customers, which was easy. I also discovered that a big chunk of Cammy's business came from online sales. She showed me how to print up the online orders, and I watched as she filled a couple. She packed them up and set them aside to be shipped out.

After that, I followed her around for the most part, listening to her handle the customer's questions with a combination of aromatherapy and herbalism all rolled into one.

In between the sales, I asked her more about how she made her bath products. It was interesting, and I hoped she meant it when she said I could help make the next batch of melt and pour soaps for Halloween.

The day rolled on with a steady stream of customers. It was peaceful and calm, and I had to get used to the idea of working someplace so damn Zen...At least that's what Id thought until a woman came in with a howling baby.

The mother was desperate for some type of natural remedy. She pounced on Cammy before the door closed. What started out as a discussion on product soon morphed in to something else.

Something that surprised me.

"I have a very gentle lavender lotion suitable for infants," Cammy said, pitching her voice over the baby's crying. "It may help her wind down after her bath in the evenings."

I stayed busy dusting and straightening the lower shelves against the back wall, while shamelessly eavesdropping on their conversation.

"By the goddess," the mother said. "I'll totally try that tonight, but nothing is working on this diaper rash, and Luna is miserable."

"Oh, poor baby girl," Cammy said, taking the baby from the frazzled mother's arms.

"I've tried everything," the young mother said. "Prescriptions, store bought ointments, and *nothing* is working, in fact, it seems to be getting worse!"

"I think I have something that may help." Cammy put the baby over her shoulder and went over to fetch a short glass jar.

"This whole new mother thing is more stressful than the haunted houses we used to investigate back in college." The mother said with a tired laugh.

Haunted houses? I thought.

"This is my own blend of diaper cream. It's all natural, and an old family recipe," Cammy explained, passing the jar to the woman. "I make this with coconut oil, beeswax, shea butter, and essential lavender oil."

While the mother considered it, Cammy rubbed circles on the baby's back and her crying began to subside.

"Lavender oil is protective, and it's supposed to be excellent for healing," the mother said.

"Yes, it is. My sister swears by this diaper cream." Cammy nodded. "She uses it on my six-month old niece, Danielle."

The baby let out a shuddering sigh and was quiet.

"You always did have the magick touch." The mother smiled as her baby dropped her head on Cammy's shoulder. "Whatever charm you just used on her, please teach it to me."

My breath rushed out. *Magick touch? Charm?*

Cammy smiled and passed the baby back. "Luna's simply picking up on your frustrated and tired vibes, Dawn…but I can enchant the cream so it works faster, if you'd like."

"Absolutely!" Dawn smiled.

"The least I can do is to help out a fellow witch-sister in need."

When I heard the word *witch*, I bobbled the jar of lotion I'd been pretending to dust. I rescued it, but the jar rapped hard against the shelf.

Cammy slid her eyes over toward me and smiled.

I put my face back into what I hoped was a casual expression and, resolutely, went back to my dusting.

After the woman, Dawn, and her baby left, Cammy sauntered over to me. "I suppose you have a few questions about what you overheard."

"A few." I cleared my throat.

"Let me start by saying that the daughters of Midnight are descended from a long line of wise women and herbalists."

"Wise women?" I asked. "Is that like Wicca or something?"

Cammy nodded. "Yes and no. The path of the wise woman is a healing path and over the centuries there was a time when we were persecuted for it."

"Persecuted?" I tipped my head to one side. "Are we talking about the burning times?"

Cammy smiled. "You know your history."

"I took a women's studies class once at the community center. It was fascinating, and empowering. It also totally pissed off my mother."

"Which probably only made you even *more* curious," Cammy guessed. "Did you study anything else?"

"I went to some free Wicca discussion groups at a New Age shop in Bakersfield. It was kinda cool. They touched on magickal herbalism a bit..." I trailed off when Cammy started to grin. I shrugged. "I guess I sound foolish."

"No, not at all." Cammy said. "This is your heritage too."

"I figured you'd all probably think it was dumb. After being around Dru in the garden and listening to you all day, it's pretty clear that I know next to nothing."

"Everyone has to start somewhere."

I brushed a strand of hair away from my face. “I suppose that’s true.”

“You are a daughter of Midnight,” Cammy said. “I’m not surprised that you found a way to learn despite being separated from your family.”

“Everything happens for a reason, I guess.”

Cammy winked. “Exactly.”

“Your friend who was just in?” I asked. “You knew her from college?”

“Dawn and I were part of a paranormal investigation team while we were in grad school.”

I blinked at how casually she’d said that. “That’s interesting.”

Cammy laughed. “That’s what folks say when they’re nervous but don’t know how to respond. Like magick, the topic of ghosts can freak people out.”

I put my hands on my hips. “You’re telling me that you’ve actually seen a ghost? A real ghost?”

“Of course. There are a lot of legends about monsters and ghosts around here.” Cammy fluffed her pink hair. “Did you know that Alton,

Illinois is considered one of the most haunted places in America?"

Note to self, I thought. *Look up Alton's haunted history.* "That makes me feel *so* much better," I said dryly. "Spook central is only twenty miles down the river road..."

Cammy grinned at my tone. "Let me tell you about what Jacob and I experienced up at the mansion on Notch Cliff last year."

I pulled up a stool behind the counter and listened as Cammy told me about how she'd first seen the ghost when she'd been a girl, and how she had recently played out her part in a family prophecy involving the haunting. I was fascinated as she described how she and her fiancé, Jacob, and his little boy Jaime had all interacted with the ghosts in the old mansion, and how they'd eventually solved the mystery of what had happened to his ancestor's dowry.

"All that happened in the same house where Gabriella and Philippe live with their baby?" I asked.

"Yes." Cammy nodded. "It's a part of the winery that Philippe and Garrett own, and Philippe has completely renovated the house.

The majority of it serves as an event venue these days."

"Oh." I started to connect the dots. "That's what Drusilla was talking about when she said the wedding was being held at Philippe's place at the winery."

"It's a gorgeous, gothic old house," Cammy said. "Wait until you see it tomorrow night."

I shuddered. "I can hardly wait."

"You'll get a chance to take it all in at the rehearsal dinner. But I don't want you to worry." Cammy rested a hand on my shoulder. "The haunting seems to have settled down since the amethysts were returned to the Ames' family."

"The bride that disappeared? Did they ever find her body?"

"Nope." Cammy shook her head. "No one knows what actually happened to Bridgette Ames-Marquette."

"Her husband, he was the main suspect, you said?"

"He was." Cammy nodded. "But he died six months after Bridgette disappeared."

"That's harsh," I said. "Poor dude was forced

into a marriage with someone he didn't love, and then his wife disappeared. Sounds like he had a miserable life."

Cammy walked over to a set of shelves and began rearranging things. "Most people aren't very sympathetic to Pierre-Michel when they hear the tale."

Pierre-Michel. All the hair on the back of my neck rose up. *Why did that name seem familiar to me?*

"There's a portrait of him up at the mansion," Cammy said, as she re-worked the display of bath bombs in metal pails. "Philippe uncovered the painting during the renovations and Gabriella put it and old family papers and documents on display in a room at the mansion for people to see. The history room is a popular tourist stop now, especially with the winery so close."

"I suppose everybody loves a good ghost story." I went over to help her. "Plus, it's a good way to tease the newbies in town—like me."

"I'd *never* tease you about something like that," Cammy insisted. "Especially when I'm pretty damn sure that you are a part of another

Midnight family prophecy, yourself."

I frowned. "What are you talking about?"

"While I was trying to solve the mystery of the missing dowry, Gran gave me an old book that was filled with one of our ancestor's writings. She had written dozens of poems and spells—"

"Spells?"

Cammy kept right on speaking. "—And a prophecy about the *four stars of Midnight*."

My jaw dropped. "Are you serious?"

"Our ancestor spoke of a 'lost star' finding her way home."

"*Madre de dios*," I breathed, and reached for my pendant for comfort.

"Originally, I believed that it was another rambling poem, but after Gran dropped the bombshell about us having another sister, I realized that it was, in fact, written about you."

"It can't be." I shook my head. "Written about me—that is."

"I'm betting it is." Cammy winked. "The prophecy spoke of a lost *star*. Isn't your name, Spanish for star?" she asked.

It was. I caught myself fiddling with my

necklace and I dropped it against my shirt. “I’d like to see that prophecy for myself.”

“Sure thing.” Cammy smiled. “As soon as the wedding craziness is over, we can sit down and read it together.”

CHAPTER FOUR

My conversation with Cammy had given me plenty to think about. It was sort of interesting that I'd been drawn to women's studies and magick, and my father's family had been practicing herbalism for generations.

The night of the rehearsal dinner, I wore the borrowed black dress and added my own black, ankle-length boots. They weren't new, but I had taken a permanent marker to the minor scuffs, and it made the damage disappear. I turned the outfit funkier by layering my denim jacket over the dress. I let my blue goldstone pendant lie on top of the bodice and called it good.

Drusilla had been picked up by Garrett, Cammy was going with her fiancé, and I ended up riding along to the mansion with Priscilla.

We drove up the winding cliff road and I discovered that I was feeling a bit anxious. By the time we'd reached the summit and pulled onto the drive that led to the event parking lot, my heart was pounding.

"Is everything all right, dear?" my grandmother asked.

I nodded, unable to speak as I studied the building. The stone house seemed familiar, which made me uneasy, and that put me on edge.

"Estella?" She studied me from across the roof of the car.

I flashed her a smile. "I guess the ghost stories Cammy told me are making me nervous after all."

My grandmother chuckled. "Don't worry. The house is quiet these days."

I fell in step with her. As we walked inside the massive stone home, I gave myself a silent lecture about not letting my imagination run away with me.

We were greeted by Gabriella, who ushered us to the ballroom where the reception would be held. Already, the tables were in place and covered with ivory tablecloths. There were a few vendors setting up too. The florist was currently placing centerpieces on the tables.

"Aren't the flowers pretty?" Gabriella said when she noticed me checking them out.

"What are these big white ones?" I asked, running a fingertip over the blossom.

Gabriella explained they were hydrangeas, and I liked the way they looked with the other green flowers, lacy ferns and slender twigs. Another worker was going behind the florist, placing candleholders and table numbers on the tables. I smiled when I saw that the small wooden plaques were framed out by green moss. *Very enchanted garden looking,* I thought, and was impressed that they were getting a jump on things for tomorrow.

There was happy chattering from the family, and I was content to stay in the background and observe as the event coordinator took the bridal party outside to walk through the ceremony.

I sat off to one side on a low stone wall, pulled my jacket closer and tried not to be in the way.

That plan lasted for about a minute and a half

before I found myself holding the baby while her parents practiced their roles as bridesmaid and best man.

I held the baby up and under her arms while she stood testing out her feet on my lap. She stared at me very seriously but didn't smile.

"Sorry about this, Danielle," I said. "I was the only one with free hands, so you got stuck with me."

The baby was less than impressed with my apology and began to fuss. I stood up, tucked her on my hip, and began to walk with her back and forth across the courtyard. I could see from my vantage point that the back gardens were more formal, and I admired the gravel pathways, solar lighting, young hedges, and a scattering of flowers. "See the lighting bugs, Danielle?" I asked, pointing across the gardens.

I could make out a pair of ornate metal gates and stone walls. I was curious enough about the grounds to almost go and walk through the flowers and the fireflies, but I didn't imagine Gabriella would be comfortable with someone she barely knew being out of eyesight with her infant.

Danielle seemed happy so long as we were on the move, so I contented myself with staying on the terrace. "What's it like living in this big spooky old house, *princesa*?" I eyeballed the tower on the far eastern side of the home. "Is your room up there like Sleeping Beauty's?"

Slowly, Danielle started to smile, and then babble and coo in response to my words.

"Is that right?" I said. "Tell me all about it."

Danielle bounced, squealed and grabbed ahold of my long hair. She decided to sample it for herself and I gently removed it from her chubby fist. She latched on to my star pendant next and I let her pull on that, until she tried to put it into her mouth. I would gently stop her… which only made her smile at me and try again.

"Nope, sorry," I said, taking it out of her mouth.

Danielle gave me a solemn stare in reply.

"She's stubborn, like her mother," Philippe's voice carried to me as he walked over.

"She looks like you," I said to the Frenchman. "Except for the blue eyes."

Philippe smiled. "I think that she favors her mother."

I passed my hand over the baby's head as I considered that. "Her hair is wavy like Gabriella's, but it's dark like yours."

"It's almost exactly the same shade and texture as yours," Gabriella said, joining us.

Not sure how to respond to that, I immediately passed the baby back to her mother.

"Looks like you, me, and the baby all inherited Dad's wavy hair," Gabriella said, casually. "Genetics are a funny thing."

I smiled. "Probably."

Gabriella hitched the baby higher on the hip of her soft and floating floral dress. "I'm sorry I haven't had much of an opportunity to come see you and get to know you better in the past few days. But we've been crazy busy getting the ballroom and terraces ready for Dru and Garrett's wedding."

I tucked my hands in my jacket pockets. "I understand."

"So, what do you think of the mansion?" Gabriella asked.

"Great atmosphere. I like the gardens," I answered politely.

"Dru and I worked on them this summer," Gabriella said. "We planted wildflowers and native plants along the pathways. They'll be easier to take care of in the long run."

I nodded at her explanation as the event coordinator called for everyone to go back inside.

Philippe made an 'after you' gesture and I fell in step with the family. "We'll give you a tour after dinner." Philippe smiled as he spoke, but I found the idea of walking around the old house held zero appeal to me.

My stomach was tight, and I recognized the feeling in the pit of my stomach as dread, which I simply did not understand. Feeling chilled, I left my denim jacket on during dinner. I noticed everyone else seemed fine, but I figured it was me adapting to the new mid-western climate.

The dinner itself was set up in a smaller banquet room, and I ended up seated at a table with Max Dubois from the nursery and his wife Nicole.

I chatted with them easily, and after the dinner was over I took the first chance I had and escaped from the house. Going back the way I'd come in, I made my way across the terrace, down the stone steps and headed toward that big ornamental gate. The gate was noiseless when I pushed it open and with a sigh of relief, I started down the first gravel path.

Rolling my neck against the tension that had gathered in my shoulders, I walked along with the lightning bugs for company. I wandered, admiring the pretty flowers that grew along the pathway. I bent to sniff at a cluster of flowers and patted the heads of the tall purple daisy-looking flowers. *Coneflowers, purple coneflowers*, I remembered the name with pleasure. I smiled as several fireflies flew lazily around me. Suddenly, my gut tightened and my head snapped up.

I wasn't alone.

It wasn't noise that tipped me off, it was more of a feeling. Slowly I straightened and scanned the area. I spotted the man standing in the shadows of the house and watched as he began to walk toward me. After years of working at bars, I knew how to spot someone who didn't belong. The man walked forward with his head high and as if he owned the place...but it was his gait that wasn't quite right. He was limping.

One of his legs dragged ever so slightly behind him and occasionally it would scuff in the gravel. I didn't recognize him from the rehearsal dinner guests, but he didn't strike me as someone who was out of place. With a ball cap tugged over his hair, jeans and gray Henley shirt, I figured he was likely an employee taking a break.

"Hello," I said.

"Good evening." His voice had a slight British accent. "Are you here with the wedding rehearsal party?"

"Yes." I nodded. "Are you taking a break?"

He tipped the brim of his cap back. "A break?"

"From the wedding reception set-up," I clarified.

His jaw set beneath a short, stubble beard. "Do I look like the hired help?"

His snide tone of voice and offended attitude surprised me. "I didn't see you with the wedding party," I said. "I assumed you were part of the event crew."

"Hardly." He looked down his nose at me. "Not that it's any of your business, but I live here." He started to walk away.

"I doubt that," I called after him. "This is Gabriella and her husband's house."

He kept right on walking, but his voice carried clearly. "Not quite."

Pendejo, I thought. The man walked off and disappeared into the shadows, and I wondered what he meant by that parting comment. In the distance, I heard my name being called. Turning, I walked out of the gardens, back up the stone steps, and made my way to the terrace.

Gabriella stood waiting for me. "How about that tour?"

I managed to smile. "Sure."

Gabriella hooked her arm through mine and led the way back inside.

They certainly were a touchy-feely bunch, I thought.

As we walked down the main hallway on the first floor past the ballroom, and next the smaller banquet room that was being used for the rehearsal, she told me about the renovations that had been done to the old family home. We traveled farther away from the party, past a bar area, public restrooms and what appeared to be an office. Gabriella opened a door to a room on the right and I stepped in with her.

"This is the room I made into a sort of mini-museum," she said. "It features the history of the founding families of Ames Crossing. The Marquettes of course, and the Ames family as well."

I scanned the cases filled with vintage photos, small antiques, some papers, and a few old newspaper clippings. There was also a large copy of an old photo of the Marquette mansion as it had appeared in the mid 1800's.

Casually I glanced around the rest of the room, doing my best to appear as if I was interested. When I saw the portrait hanging on the wall, I stopped cold. There was *something* about it...

"This is the portrait of Pierre-Michel Marquette," Gabriella said.

"How old is the painting?" I heard myself ask.

"Circa 1840," she said. "Pierre-Michel was

Philippe's great-great-great uncle."

I nodded at her words and stepped closer to the painting. A striking man stared back from the portrait. He stood with the Marquette Mansion in the background, as it must have been a very long time ago.

I didn't know a damn thing about art, but the image appeared so real that it read almost like a photograph. Carefully, I studied the face of the man in the portrait. He'd been young when he'd had his portrait painted, late teens or early twenties, I guessed. His hair was dark and fell to his shoulders. It framed a lean, attractive face with sharp cheekbones. His eyes were poetically large, dark, and they dominated his face. He was attractive I supposed...in an old-world sort of way.

"This painting isn't exactly my favorite piece of the Marquette family history," Gabriella said.

"Yeah," I agreed. "It has some creepy vibes coming from it, for sure."

Gabriella moved a tad closer to me, until we were standing with our shoulders brushing. "That's almost word-for-word what I said to Philippe the first time I saw the painting."

I slid my eyes over to her face and saw she was serious.

Gabriella shrugged. “The old portrait used to be in our family wing, but it made me uncomfortable, so we moved it down here.”

“I don’t blame you,” I said. “This is the guy that was accused of killing his wife, right?”

Gabriella raised her eyebrows. “I suppose Cammy told you about the history of the house, and the dowry that had been missing for almost two hundred years?”

I crossed my arms, feeling a sudden chill. “Cammy was telling me about her college ghost hunting days, and that led to her filling me in on how she and Jacob had found his ancestor’s missing jewelry in your house.”

“I know it all sounds fantastic,” Gabriella said. “But it honestly did happen.” She turned to her right and pointed. “Look over here. The Ames family has allowed us to have part of Bridgette’s amethyst parure permanently on display here in the museum room.”

I followed where she pointed and saw a gorgeous amethyst bracelet inside of a glass case. Next to it was a black and white photo of

Bridgette Ames wearing the entire set of jewelry. "Wow," I breathed, looking at the deep purple stones.

"We took the original daguerreotype of Bridgette and her sister, cropped it and had a larger copy framed and made for the display here," Gabriella explained.

"Bridgette Ames," I said, taking in the sober expression on the young woman's face. My mouth had gone bone dry, and it took real effort to keep my voice even. "She didn't look very happy."

"At the time, it wasn't the style to smile for your photograph," Gabriella said. "But I agree, she looked like a very unhappy young woman."

She seemed sort of sour to me, I thought.

"Look here." Gabriella tapped on the glass case. "See these letters? They are from Claude, Pierre-Michele's brother. He wrote what he'd known about Bridgette and his brother and had tucked the letter in with the jewelry case when he hid them."

While Gabriella explained what was in the letters, I couldn't help but study the portrait of Pierre-Michel, and my heart rapped hard against my ribs. There was something about him, and I found it both compelling and disturbing all at the same time.

It didn't make any sense...but I couldn't shake the feeling that I knew him.

"There you are!" Cammy appeared in the doorway and I jumped hard. "Sorry to interrupt," she said.

"That's okay," Gabriella said.

I shifted my attention to Cammy. Her dress tonight was short, made of black lace and snug—even more so than mine. "Come on you two, Drusilla wants to get a few family pictures before the rehearsal dinner ends."

I stepped back even as Gabriella moved forward. "You two go ahead," I said.

"Don't be ridiculous." Cammy shook her head and long, witchy, crystal earrings swung from her ears. "Dru said she wanted photos of the four of us together, specifically."

Her heartfelt tone made me feel ungracious, and I guiltily glanced from Gabriella to Cammy. "I'm not used to having relatives." I tried to explain to them.

"Relatives, my ass." Gabriella slipped an arm

around my shoulders. “You are *family*, Estella.”

I studied Gabriella’s blue eyes. She might look soft and pretty, but she was tough, blunt and no-nonsense. “You’re a hard-ass, aren’t you?”

“Damn straight,” Gabriella answered.

I couldn’t help the snort of laughter. “Good. It makes me like you better.”

Gabriella threw back her head and laughed. The two flanked me as we walked back to the rehearsal dinner and I told myself to put my reaction to that old painting out of my mind. My discomfort had to be due to the new surroundings.

There was no way that man in the painting could be familiar to me. It was simply a case of nerves and jet lag, I told myself firmly.

That’s all it could be.

***

The next afternoon, I sat beside my grandmother in the front row on the bride’s side, watching as my oldest sister spoke her wedding vows. The stone terrace had been decorated with big pots of white hydrangeas, ferns, and an arbor that was drenched in white and pale green flowers. With twinkling lights and candles, it all had the appearance of a faery tale.

I hadn't been to very many weddings, but I liked Dru's ivory gown that she'd chosen. The fabric of the skirt was sheer and flowing—chiffon, Priscilla had said. The bodice of the dress had a deep V-neck, was lacy, and had cap sleeves. When I'd peeked in on Dru before the ceremony had begun, I'd noticed that the lace details on the shoulders of the gown were teeny tiny flowers made from sheer ivory fabric.

Brooke stood up for the couple as the maid of honor, and Gabriella and Cammy were the bridesmaids. The attendants' dresses were a sage green made of matte satin. They were knee length and featured a deep V-neckline with a bit of pleating at the bodice. Brooke's dress was the same fabric and color as the bridesmaids, but with a scoop neckline—more suitable for a girl her age. The bouquets were simple but romantic, with cream-colored roses, airy ferns, pale green hydrangeas and tied with a wide navy-blue satin ribbon.

The men were looking sharp in navy tuxes, white shirts, and sage green ties. I scanned the attire of the rest of the wedding guests and was very glad Cammy had let me borrow the navy sequined dress. People were dressed to impress, and next to Priscilla's deep blue lace dress, I sort of matched the color scheme of sage and navy—almost as if I belonged.

I wiggled my toes in the slightly too large black pumps I'd borrowed from Dru, and saw that Priscilla was crying, happy tears. I fished inside of her handbag myself and passed her a tissue. "Here you go."

The smile she flashed was brilliant, and she took my hand and gave it a squeeze. "I'm so glad you are here."

"Me too," I whispered automatically. As the bride and groom sealed the deal with a kiss, I realized that I was genuinely happy to be there.

Later, the reception was in full swing and I was sitting at the bar, waiting for my drink. I was chatting up Jacob as the bartender poured a glass of white wine for my grandmother and a shot of Patrón for me.

"Damn, girl," Jacob laughed as I tossed back the shot and picked up the lime wedge.

"What?" I asked and sucked on the lime. "I told you, I'm a bartender, I can handle my alcohol."

I picked up the glass of white Priscilla had requested and turned to take it over to her. Easing my way through the people standing two-deep at the bar, I bumped solidly into a man. "Damn it," I swore under my breath, and barely managed to keep the drink from sloshing all over the man's dinner jacket.

"I beg your pardon," he said, steadying me with one hand.

I was about to apologize, and when I glanced up, scowled instead. "You!" It was the rude guy I'd spoken to in the gardens the night before.

He tipped his head politely, but the lopsided grin was more sneer than smile. "Hello, again."

Taking a swift assessment of his dark, expensive suit, I sized up my opponent. I knew he hadn't been at the rehearsal the night before...so who was he? Before I could ask, Cammy appeared at my side. "Hey Estella, I don't think you've had the chance to meet

Chauncey."

I frowned over the name. "Shawn C?"

"Chauncey Marquette," Cammy said with a smile.

"Charmed," he said with the slightest of bows.

"This is Philippe's brother," Cammy explained.

"Half-brother," Chauncey added.

"Chauncey, I'd like to introduce you to my sister, Estella." Cammy made the introduction smoothly.

"We've met," I said, tersely.

"In the walled gardens last night," Chauncey said to Cammy.

"Perfect," she said with a smile. "You know, Chauncey, Estella hasn't danced yet."

"Camilla." I tried to wave that off.

"Oh?" Chauncey gave her a bland smile.

"I think you should ask her to dance." Cammy batted her eyes innocently.

"It would be my pleasure." His tone was perfectly polite, but his expression made it clear to me that he was about as thrilled with the suggestion as I was.

I held up the wine glass. "But I was going to —"

"I'll take this to Gran." Cammy nipped the glass of wine out of my hand. "You two go enjoy the music." With a firm hand, she nudged us both toward the dance floor.

"For god's sake," I grumbled.

"I suppose we both just got maneuvered," he said, and escorted me out to join the other dancers.

With a sigh, I accepted his right hand, and formally rested my left on his shoulder. "Let's get this over with."

His lips twitched at my words even as we began to slow dance. "How do you like Ames Crossing?" he asked a few moments later.

I stared over his shoulder. "I like it fine."

"Are you enjoying yourself this evening?" he said.

"I was until a minute ago," I said, wryly.

He laughed at my comeback and when I shifted my eyes to his, everything tilted.

The room slid away, and I found myself surrounded by people dressed in clothes from a different time period. Instead of a DJ, there was a piano playing in the background and the man who held me in his arms, was the same, but he was also different.

His hair was longer, and his face was younger and clean-shaven. Yet his dark eyes, and the expression in them, were eerily the same.

He'd asked me if I was enjoying myself once before, I realized. But that had been a long, long time ago...

In another life.

The thought snapped me back, and suddenly, everything returned to the present—as it should be.

Chauncey Marquette was staring at me. "Estella," he said, and his fingers tightened slightly on my mine to get my attention. "Are you all right?"

Totally shaken by what had happened, I stepped back from him. "Excuse me," I said. The music changed to a faster tempo, and taking the opportunity for a quick escape, I walked away.

CHAPTER FIVE

I went directly to my grandmother, sat, and kept her company at the family table. She was speaking to the Dubois', who were showing off photos of their baby boy, Caleb. I stayed by her side and wondered what in the hell was going on with me. I knew it wasn't the tequila shot, but damn, I was switching to water for the rest of the night.

Brooke, I noted, was bopping around the reception, and the girl was actually smiling. She'd pulled all of my sisters out on the dance floor and they were dancing to Whitney Houston's, *I Wanna Dance With Somebody*. She appeared to be having a wonderful time.

Over the next half hour I was introduced to several new people, including Cammy's future in-laws, and I did my best to commit their names to memory. While the conversation flowed around me, I sat back and observed Philippe's brother interact with the other wedding guests.

I had no idea why that little episode had happened when I had danced with him. But I damn sure didn't like it, and it made me very suspicious. I watched him for a while, figuring he had to be the reason for it all.

Dude had some slick moves, I thought as he worked the crowd. The limp I'd noticed before wasn't in evidence tonight. He brushed a careless hand over the shoulder of a woman, smiling down into her face, and I thought she might pass out from the attention. She had been shamelessly flirting with him, and for a moment it looked like it had worked out for her. I had to smother a laugh when she lost his attention only a short time later. She'd pouted over it and flounced off when Chauncey had turned away to chat with a group of men.

Which made me realize as I watched, that the schmooze came naturally to him.

Sure, he was good-looking, but it was a

polished kind of style, almost magazine photo-shoot slick. My gut said he was a player, and I'd seen enough of that type of false suave-ness with the male upper brass in the Air Force to last me a lifetime.

I sipped at my glass of water and continued to watch him, even when he exchanged a brief word with Gabriella. She laughed happily over something he'd said. Gabriella seemed to care about him. It was obvious. When Philippe joined their talk a few moments later, the married couple linked hands and leaned into each other as they spoke to the man.

After tending bar for so many years I knew how to read body language. Gabriella and Philippe were sincerely in love, and they considered the other man family. It was as simple as that.

With a sigh, I excused myself from the table and went to go use the ladies' room. I needed a break and a brisk walk to shake the dregs off from whatever the hell that 'snapshot of the past' thing had been.

I was on my way back to the reception when I had the bad luck to run into him again.

"Shawn," I said deliberately, nodding as I passed him.

"It's Chauncey," he said, exaggerating the pronunciation with a French accent.

"*Carrajo*" I shook my head.

"No, that's not how you say it." He appeared completely serious.

It was on the tip of my tongue to tell him I'd just called him a 'dick,' but I considered my surroundings. "Do you have a problem?" I asked instead.

"Not as much as you appear to have a chip on your shoulder."

I planted my hands on my hips. "You don't even know me."

"It's not easy being an outsider, is it?"

My stomach clenched. I got the weirdest feeling of déjà vu. As if he'd said that to me once before.

The Midnights seemed genuinely fond of him, and with that in mind, I took a deep breath and chose not to respond to his taunt. Determined not to let him know that he affected me, I tossed my head and started to move past him. Clearly something was off with me tonight, and it wouldn't be my best move to antagonize my sister and brother-in-law's relative.

"Gabriella has spoken of you," he said.

I stopped, turned on my heel, and considered him. "And?"

"I've only lived here for a few months myself. I know it can be challenging when you are trying to adapt to a completely different lifestyle."

"Umm hmm." I nodded and yet despite myself, was curious. "Your accent is strange. Where are you from?"

"Well, you *are* charming, aren't you?" he said. It wasn't a compliment.

"I *meant*, that I can't pinpoint where you're from. Sometimes you sound French, like Philippe, and other times I pick up a British accent. So, what gives with that?"

"My mother is British, and my father is French."

I nodded. "Ah, I knew I heard some Brit in your tone." So much for polite conversation. I took a step to leave.

His voice stopped me. "Gabriella tells me

you're from California?"

I shrugged. "I'm from all over, military brat. But California is the last place I lived."

"I lived in Europe for the past several years...traveled, you could say, for my job. It was a definite culture shock moving here."

"Europe, eh? Sounds pretty fancy," I said, dryly.

Chauncey shrugged. "It had its moments."

"What made you give up the fast life for Ames Crossing, Illinois?"

His shoulders stiffened. "I guess you could say that my luck ran out." He nodded. "If you'll excuse me."

I stepped aside and he continued down the hall and toward the family wing of the house. I watched as he slipped a key card from his pants pocket and swiped it. The door closed behind him with a definite thud.

Once he was gone, I blew out a shaky breath. "Weird," I decided. I headed back to the reception and tried to recall if I'd ever had such strange reactions to a person or a place before.

I moved past the museum room and hesitated in the doorway. I studied that old portrait of

Pierre-Michel, and felt the hair rise on the back of my neck. "You're creepy," I said to the painting. It felt like he was staring at me, and deliberately, I turned my back on the portrait, left the room, and went to go find my relatives.

***

The day after the wedding was quiet. I was a tad uncomfortable when I realized that Brooke was coming to stay with us at the farmhouse while Garrett and Drusilla went on their honeymoon. Brooke made herself at home in Dru's room and was bubbly and animated as she spoke to Priscilla and Cammy. To me she nodded without so much as a smile.

To give us both some space, I took my book on herbs outside and walked around the gardens, trying to identify as many plants as possible. Come Monday, I wanted to show Cammy that I had been studying. That, and I figured it would be best to stay clear of the tween.

When Gabriella called inviting me to come over for dinner, I pounced on the idea. I tossed my denim jacket over my t-shirt and jeans, brushed out my hair and touched up my face. I brushed a bit more copper on my eyelids, added more mascara, and cleaned up my eyeliner so it was more of a proper smoky eye—as opposed to casually smudged.

Priscilla let me borrow the old family truck, and it was a quick drive to the *Trois Amis* winery. I parked the car in the winery parking lot and hoofed it up the landscaped hill to the Marquette mansion.

The young trees were brushed with a hint of red, and I stopped to admire them. I was pretty sure some of the trees were oaks, but I wasn't sure about the others. Making a mental note to ask Gabriella about it, I walked to the private entrance on the farthest eastern side of the house.

I'd been told to walk right in, and I did. I'd barely shut the door behind me when Gabriella appeared at the top of the stairs. Like me, she was wearing jeans and a shirt. She was also holding her daughter on her hip. "Finally!" she said. "I have you all to myself."

"Hey there," I said, and started up the stairs.

We ended up in the tower room, which I came to discover they used as a sort of library or den.

The room was paneled in dark wood and boasted a stone fireplace, thick mantle, and shelves of books. While the décor was on the formal side, it had been softened by potted plants on the hearth, framed baby photos, and candles on a console table. A large wedding portrait of Gabriella and Philippe was displayed above the mantle.

"Thanks for inviting me to supper," I said as we took a seat on her leather sofa.

"Did you enjoy the wedding yesterday?" She tucked Danielle on her lap, and the baby began to bounce and babble.

"I did." I nodded. "I met a bunch of new people and visited with Max and Nicole."

"Max and I have been friends for years." Gabriella pulled her long blonde hair over one shoulder.

"I visited his nursery with Dru the other day. He mentioned that Nicole is the PR person for the winery."

"I'm sure Max was showing off pictures of Caleb last night," Gabriella predicted.

I smiled. "He had a few dozen on his cell phone." I pointed to the wedding photo. "I'm digging that blue wedding gown you wore."

Gabriella smiled. "Thanks. It was a special day for us."

"So how long have you been married?"

"A little over three months."

I did the math. Baby Danielle was six months. Before I could ask about it, Gabriella was continuing...

"If Philippe would have had his way we'd have been married before Danielle was born, but I refused to wear a maternity gown to my own wedding."

I chuckled at that. "How did you two meet?"

"Here, at a masquerade party for the winery."

"Really?"

I listened, fascinated, as Gabriella told me the story of how she and Philippe had met, fallen in love, become parents and eventually married.

"Oh, I get it. The blue gown was a nod to how you met?"

"Yes, and to the night Danielle was conceived." Gabriella laughed as the baby started to squirm. "Just goes to show that even a wise woman doesn't always know everything, or what fate has in store for her."

"Camilla was telling me about the family traditions," I began.

"Watch yourself or you'll be spell casting under the next full moon with her." Gabriella winked.

I smiled. "You might be shocked to know I've done some casting in my time."

Gabriella's eyebrows rose. "No kidding?"

"I attended some workshops on Wicca in California."

She bounced the baby on her knee. "Magick tends to find a way. Did you tell Cammy about that?"

I nodded. "Yup."

"By the goddess, I bet she was *thrilled*."

Danielle reached over toward me and before I had time to react, Gabriella was passing the baby. I sat the baby in my lap and she immediately grabbed for my star pendant and began to gnaw on it.

"Danielle likes you," Gabriella said.

I snuggled the baby a bit closer. "She's super

cute."

"And stubborn." Gabriella nodded.

"It is my curse to have stubborn females in my life," Philippe said from the doorway.

I saw that he was grinning. "Yeah, you look like you're suffering."

"Hello, Estella." He came into the room, dressed more casually than I'd seen him before, and sat in a club chair. "I'm glad you were able to join us tonight."

"No. Thank you," I said. "Brooke is staying at the farmhouse for a week and she's pretty suspicious of me. I was relieved when you invited me to supper."

Philippe rubbed a hand over his chin. "Brooke has been through much in her young life. She is slow to trust."

"Priscilla told me about Brooke," I said. "I understand better than most that it's tough to lose your parents at such a young age."

A musical alert sounded, and Gabriella pulled her phone out of her pocket and clicked off the alarm. "Chicken stew should be done." She stood. "Let's go down to the kitchen."

I carried the baby downstairs to the family

kitchen and tucked her in her high chair. While Gabriella dished up her chicken stew and put some bread in a napkin-lined basket, Philippe began to feed the baby. I took my seat and was thoroughly entertained by watching Danielle eat her baby food.

I started to laugh when the baby gave her father the raspberries and sprayed him with strained peas. “It’s dinner and a show,” I said, while Philippe laughed and wiped up the high chair tray.

Suddenly, I noticed there were four places set at the old dining table. *Who else was joining us?* I wondered.

“There you are,” Gabriella said to someone behind me.

My stomach dropped. It was Chauncey.

“You said five thirty,” he said as he pulled out a chair and sat beside me.

Terrific, I thought. *Of course, he’d park his butt right next to me.*

“Did you wash your hands?” Gabriella asked him as she placed the bowls on the table.

“Yes, Mum.” Chauncey shook his head.

“How goes the punch list for the suites?”

Philippe asked.

"Down to the touch-up painting." Chauncey smiled and reached for the basket of biscuits. "The cleaning crew should be able to begin in a few days."

Gabriella took her seat. "The hotel suites are almost finished," she said to me from across the table. "We should be ready for business by October!"

I tried to recall what she'd told me when she'd given me a tour of the house. "You said there were going to be a half dozen rooms, right?"

"Yes," Philippe said. "Chauncey investing in the family business has allowed us to finish up the renovations to the western wing *much* quicker than we ever dreamed."

"Are you in hotel management?" I asked Chauncey.

He smiled. "I am now."

Danielle started to bang her hands on the high chair tray and squealed for attention. Yes," I said, smiling at her. "You are adorable, *mija*."

Chauncey spooned up some stew. "Taking

over the hotel part of the business, was about the last thing I expected, but the job does have its benefits." He wiggled his eyebrows at the baby, making her laugh. "Like the one wearing strained peas."

The rest of the dinner passed easily enough. Chauncey was more relaxed and easier going around Gabriella, Philippe and the baby. After the meal, Philippe started on the dishes and Gabriella put the baby in the tub. When Philippe suggested that Chauncey show me the new hotel suites, I'm sure he thought it was a great idea, but being alone with Chauncey was about the last thing I wanted.

Realizing I couldn't refuse without looking bitchy, I told myself to suck it up and followed Chauncey down to the main level. *There was no reason to be nervous,* I lectured myself. *It had been the drinks and the strain of the wedding that had made me imagine all that stuff before.*

"Will we be interrupting any events?" I asked, trying to sound polite as he used that key card to access the public side of the house.

"No. The cleanup crew was finished late last

night and we're clear until Friday."

I followed him down the hallway, and to the entrance of the museum room. We'd only cleared the door when there was a large bang. "What the hell was that?" he said, stepping protectively in front of me.

Amused at the maneuver, I went around him and walked to the door to see for myself. The museum room was empty of people, and as I scanned the interior I saw that the large portrait of Pierre-Michel had come off the wall. It now rested crookedly on the floor. "The painting fell down," I said. "The wall-hanger is still in place, though. Wonder why it fell?"

Chauncey walked in the room behind me and went to the portrait. He lifted it up and checked the back of the painting. Face to face with the image of Pierre-Michel my stomach dropped to my shoes, and I gasped.

"What?" Chauncey lowered the painting. "What is it?"

I swung my eyes from the old portrait and back to the face of the man who stood before me. Seeing the old painting and Chauncey side-by-side had me realizing an uncomfortable truth. "Has anybody ever told you that you're a dead ringer for your ancestor?"

He scowled and slapped the painting back on the wall with enough force that I cringed. "I hate this painting."

"I can see that." I said, watching his reaction.

"Come on," he said, and took ahold of my elbow. "Let's get out of here."

He started to pull me with him and when he did, a memory crashed over me.

I was no longer standing in the hall of the house, I was on the cliffs while thunder boomed overhead. The present slid away, leaving the copper taste of fear in my mouth. *Someone was calling my name...or was it someone else's name?* With effort, I pulled myself back to the here and now.

"Estella!" Chauncey's voice was sharp, impatient. "Hey, are you all right?"

It took me a moment to answer. This time, being alone with him had caused me to relive a nightmare, and I found I didn't care for the experience. Not at all. *Why did this keep happening?* I wondered.

"I need to get going," I said, pulling away

from him. "We'll have to do the tour another time." I immediately headed back toward the lobby and the eastern entrance of the house.

"Are you certain you are all right?" he called after me.

Even though I was getting damn sick of hearing him ask me that, I nodded. "I'm fine. Just tired. Tell Gabriella and Philippe thank you for dinner. *Buenos noches*." I kept moving, let myself out the private door, and forced myself not to run.

Once I cleared the house and my feet hit the grass, I quickened my pace. I hurried to the truck, started it up, and backed out of the parking lot. With my heart pounding, I headed down the cliff road for the farmhouse.

As I drove home, I couldn't shake the feeling that Chauncey was probably watching me drive away from some window, and I truly didn't give a rat's ass. I had bigger problems, because Pierre-Michel and Chauncey's features had both somehow melded into the face of the desperate man from my dreams.

The man who I'd run from.

The man who'd called me, Victoria.

***

Maybe it was karma from skipping out after dinner and not saying goodbye to my hosts, but I had disturbing dreams all night long. They weren't Hollywood slasher style dreams—I almost wished they were—instead they were slightly out of focus, soft and romantic. Embarrassingly romantic, and then they had turned hot and sexy.

I was sitting on a quilt in the tall emerald grass having a secluded, romantic picnic with Pierre-Michel. My dress was long, cotton, and sewn from a yellow calico. It was the favorite of all my day-dresses.

He had brought me sprays of lilacs, and their hidden message of: 'the first feelings of love,' made me sigh. It was only the two of us and a perfect afternoon. After we ate, he pulled a slim volume of poetry out of the basket. Stretching out, he laid his head in my lap and read to me.

The dream shifted, and now I was alone with him in a dark hall stealing frantic kisses and passionate caresses. I unbuttoned the silk vest he wore and boldly ran my hands up and over his linen covered chest. When he moaned at my touch, I yanked his shirt free of his trousers and explored.

"Now. Love me now, Pierre-Michel," I whispered.

He nudged me back into a window seat, and I went willingly. He joined me a second later and pushed my long skirts up and out of the way. I was crazy for him, desperate to have him inside of me, and we took each other there in the middle of a dark, deserted section of the house.

"Je t'aime, Victoria," he whispered as he slid deep inside of me.

"My love," I said, pulling him closer still.

"Je t'aime pour toujour," he said. 'I'll love you forever'...

And those words had woken me.

I bolted upright in bed, my heart racing and my body throbbing. I sat there for a few moments, absolutely mortified—not for the sex dream sequence—I mean, who doesn't enjoy a good sexy dream?

"What in the hell is going on?" I scrubbed

my hands over my face and tried to figure it out. But it didn't make sense. I'd never called someone 'my love' in my entire life! That was ridiculous! And besides, I didn't even speak French...so how come I'd known what he'd said to me—I meant to *her*?

I'd had a sex dream about a man I'd called Pierre-Michel, and he'd worn Chauncey Marquette's face.

Or maybe Chauncey had *his* face.

I dropped my head in my hands and groaned.

Something really strange was going on. The dreams, the déjà vu, and that vision of the past when I'd danced with Chauncey at the wedding, and then yesterday's little flashback...

If I didn't know any better, I'd start to think that I was seeing the past through someone else's eyes. Pierre-Michel's lover, specifically.

Victoria, he'd called her.

But who the hell was she and why was she in my head?

CHAPTER SIX

Weird dreams aside, I had a job to get to and I wasn't going to let anything screw up this opportunity. I threw myself in the shower and resolutely put the visions of the past out of my head. Today, I was opening *Lotions & Potions* with Cammy at 10:00am.

Pulling a pink t-shirt with the store's logo on it over my head, I smoothed my long hair and took a critical look at myself in the mirror. I didn't usually wear pink, but it was Cammy's signature color—what a surprise. At least it had black gothic lettering on it. Besides, I didn't think wearing my *Latina A F* shirt would be appropriate in the boutique.

The pastel shirt made me look bland and washed out. I grabbed my eyeliner from my makeup bag, found it was almost empty, and gave it a brisk shake. I thickened my eyeliner, making it more of a cat eye. “Better.” I nodded with satisfaction over the result. I pulled out my one tube of lipstick and slicked that on.

I was seriously tempted to ask Cammy if she’d consider having a black shirt with pink lettering made for me. Making a mental note to ask about that, I laced up my old tennis shoes, grabbed my bag, and headed downstairs.

Once the shop was opened, we sat on stools behind the front counter. I pulled my notebook and pen out of my bag and rested it on my knee. Cammy had promised to teach me more about herbalism today, and my sister wasted no time getting started.

“The path of the wise woman, is a quiet, peaceful one,” she began. “The practice of herbal magick is both an art and a science.”

“Art and science,” I repeated, and wrote notes as fast as I could.

“Magick is a sympathetic process. It works on the basis of your own personal power and the connection between all living things. This connection—vibration, or harmony is what we tap in to." Cammy hitched her chair closer to mine. "Now, to work herb magick you need to understand the energies and elemental powers within the plant life, and what their magickal properties are."

I glanced up from my notebook. "The natural elements are earth, air, fire, and water."

"Correct." Cammy smiled. "Also, herbs have planetary correspondences as well."

"Why planetary?"

"Planetary correspondences allow you to fine tune your herbal spell-work, and each day of the week corresponds to a specific astrological influence."

I flipped a page in my notebook. "Okay, so what are they?"

"Sunday," Cammy began, "is associated with —"

"The sun," I guessed.

She smiled. "Exactly. The magicks associated with solar energies include: confidence building, realizing your goals, success and wealth."

I wrote that down. "And herbs that are connected to the sun would be what?"

“There are many.” Cammy reached behind her and pulled a book off a low shelf. “But a few that are easy to remember would be: cinnamon, orange, St. John’s wort and the sunflower.”

“The sunflower is an herb?”

“Technically a plant that is used for medicine, food, flavoring, dyes, or scent, is considered to be an herb. That includes any part of the plant—the root, leaves, bark, stems, seeds or flowers.”

“By that definition the sunflower is an herb because its seeds are edible?”

“Correct.” She nodded. “There are medicinal properties to the sunflower—Latin name, *helianthus*—but commonly, culinary oil can be pressed from its seeds, the flower buds yield a yellow dye, and that’s only for a start.”

“I’m guessing if it’s a solar herb then it would be associated with the element of fire?”

“In this case, yes.”

I added that to my notes. “Besides the name, why else is the sunflower associated with the sun?”

Cammy smiled. “Well, think of its color and

shape."

"Oh." I nodded. "I guess it does look like a sun, with the yellow petals being the rays. Okay, I can see that."

"Did you know that the sunflower turns its face and follows the sun's path through the sky during the day?"

"No. I didn't." I wrote that down too. "That's kind of cool."

"Here's another fun fact for you." Cammy gave me a friendly elbow nudge. "The Incas used sunflowers to represent their Sun God. Supposedly priestesses at the temples wore sunflowers as crowns."

"So, there's a lot of lore and legend associated with the sunflower."

"You bet," Cammy said. "In the language of flowers, the sunflower symbolizes loyalty and adoration."

"The Victorians called the language of flowers, Floriography..." I murmured. Then I caught myself. *How had I known that?*

Cammy nodded her head. "That's right."

"What about lilacs?" I heard myself say. "What do they mean?"

Cammy tucked her pink hair behind one ear. “Purple lilacs signify a first love, or the first feelings of love.”

I knew it. Just like in my dream...

“Magickally, lilacs are sacred to the faeries,” Cammy continued. “Their strong scent was also used to drive ghosts out of a home.”

I frowned. “Like an exorcism or something?”

“I’d say more along the lines of a very nicely scented banishing.” Cammy handed me the book she’d pulled. “This is a reference book I keep at the shop on magickal herbalism. You’re welcome to read it between customers.”

“Thanks.” I tucked the book on my lap. “I’ll try and get all seven of the daily planetary correspondences written down in my notebook today.”

“It takes time to learn all of this,” Cammy said, dropping a hand on my shoulder. “I don’t expect you to memorize it all in one day.”

“It’s pretty cool though,” I said. “I’m enjoying it.”

“Did you still want to help me make up a few batches of melt and pour soap today?”

“Can we do that here?”

“Of course.” Cammy smiled. “There’s a microwave on the counter in the back room.”

“You can melt the soap in the microwave?”

“Sure. For small batches of melt and pour it’s more efficient.”

“What if I screw it up?”

“You won’t,” she said. “I’ve got an easy soap recipe for you to try your hand at, using a goat’s milk base and it’s all natural.”

“What are we making?”

“I thought we’d conjure up some molded soaps.” Cammy winked. “The honey-oatmeal variety sells as fast as I make it.” She bent down and pulled a pink silicone soap mold out of her tote bag. “See these new molds?”

I took the molds from Cammy. There were six squares with the word, ‘Handmade’ on the bottom of each. “These are cute.”

“Since it’s usually slow on Monday mornings, I thought we’d make a couple of small batches.” She started walking to the back.

I stood and followed her to the back room. “Besides the honey-oatmeal, what else were you wanting to make?”

“Well, since you favor the sandalwood rose,

we'll try a melt and pour, using essential oils and dried rose petals."

Cammy opened a cupboard and pulled out another silicone mold. "If we're happy with how they turn out, we'll name the soap variety after you. I think you'll like these." She handed me the soap molds and I saw they were star shaped.

"I don't recall seeing any star shaped soaps in your shop. Is this new?"

"I bought it a month ago, on a whim," she said. "Didn't know at the time that it would end up being prophetic."

***

I spent the morning working elbow-to-elbow in the kitchenette with Cammy. I'd never done anything remotely crafty, and I discovered that I liked it. The sandalwood rose was the most fun to make because she let me decide how I wanted them to smell. I ended up using a couple more drops of the sandalwood essential oil than the rose. I also added dried, crumbled rose petals from the family's garden and a tiny bit of colorant, so the soaps would be a very pale pink.

After the sandalwood/rose soaps were poured in the star-shaped molds, we allowed them to set up for an hour. I cleaned up the bowls I'd used while Cammy waited on a few customers. I transferred the notes I'd written during the making of the soap to an index card and added that to Cammy's recipe box on the back counter.

After the soaps had hardened, Cammy showed me how to pop them out of the molds, and we transferred the soaps to a freshly paper-lined shelf to cure for a few days.

Maybe it was silly, but I was damn proud of seeing all those soaps I'd made lined up in the back room. Also, they smelled terrific.

After that, all the customers that came in I rang up. Now that Cammy was confident that I could handle any sales, she headed into Alton to ship out a large order to an online customer and left me to run the shop.

I waved her off, promised to call if I had any problems, and enjoyed having the shop to myself for the afternoon. I'd been sitting behind the front counter, where I could see the comings and goings of the tourists walking up and down the street, and took more notes on the daily magickal correspondences.

I'd been at it for about an hour when I spotted a pack of girls walking down the sidewalk. They paused outside the shop, wearing matching school uniforms, and were all either looking at their phones or gabbing to each other. I shrugged and left them to it.

I'm not sure why I looked back up when I did, but I saw a flash of red hair and noticed that Brooke James was walking down the street, shoulders hunched and staring at the ground. It was a classic—please don't pick on me—type of body language. She ignored the gaggle of girls, but as soon as they'd spotted her, as one, they shifted to confront her.

"Look who's here!" A tall blonde girl jeered. "It's the freak!"

Now all four of the girls had surrounded Brooke, and I could clearly hear their jibes and taunts from inside the shop. I set my notes aside and stood.

"I heard you had to change schools because

you were too stupid to stay at the academy," said a chunky brunette.

"Well, they do have Special Education classes at public schools," said another girl. "Is that why you changed schools, Brooke?" She shoved Brooke into the fourth girl. "Because you needed to ride the short bus?"

"Leave me alone," Brooke said, trying to duck past them.

Things were rapidly getting ugly. *Come on*, *Brooke*, I thought. *Stand up for yourself!*

The tall blonde grabbed Brooke's arm. "I still owe you for getting me suspended."

"Let go of me, Clementine!" Brooke demanded, and tried to yank away.

One of the girls shoved Brooke again, and she stumbled, but managed to stay on her feet. The tall blonde threw a punch, and Brooke blocked most of it by tossing her arms up in front of her face.

I'd seen enough. As the pack of girls moved in for the kill, I marched over to the front door, yanked it open, and stepped out into the fray.

"Break it up!" I grabbed the tallest of the group by the arm and hauled her off of Brooke.

She took a swing at me, and without thinking, I moved into a preemptive arm control maneuver.

My right hand shot low for her wrist and my left grabbed her high on the triceps. Grasping the girl's arm nice and tight, I turned her arm up and back behind her. I leaned in, dropped my weight, and she immediately bent over.

"Hey!" she squealed, and struggled. "Let go of me!"

I angled my hand to the back of her head, pressed, and pushed her easily to the ground. She went face down on the sidewalk. Keeping her wrist high, I put one of my knees on her lower back and the other on the back of her neck, pinning her in place. "Everything okay, Brooke?" I asked in a pleasant tone, as the other girls jumped back.

The redhead went from pale to bright red. "Yes, I'm okay."

"Why don't you step inside the shop, while I have a heart-to-heart with your friends, here?" I suggested.

Brooke stepped back toward the door, but didn't go inside.

When the blonde began to struggle, I applied

a bit more pressure. "You girls should get gone," I said, and the other three bolted.

"Let go of me!" The blonde on the ground gasped.

"Well, I will," I said, and continued to kneel on her. "Just as soon as you calm your little bitch-ass down."

"Do you want me to do anything to help?" Brooke asked.

I glanced over at Brooke and saw the smallest of smiles was hovering on her face.

"You can call the cops," I said and that comment had the girl on the ground shrieking.

"You can't treat me like this! I'll tell my parents!"

"Won't that be fun?" I said. "I can't *wait* to show your parents and the cops the security video from the store. I know for a fact one of the cameras is aimed at the front sidewalk."

"It is?" Brooke asked.

I nodded to her and then shifted my attention back to the girl I had pinned. "I'm sure there's some nice footage of you punching Brooke, *and* of you and your three pals shoving and taunting her," I said. "I bet we could make harassment charges stick, maybe even post the video of four girls bullying and ganging up against one girl on social media..."

"Oh my god," Brooke half-laughed. "This is *awesome*."

The blonde started to cry and I stayed as I was, keeping the girl on the ground, waiting for her to calm down. "If you can promise not to do anything stupid, I'll let you up," I said. "Behave yourself, *chica* or I'll have you flat on your face again."

"Okay," she sobbed.

"Remember what I said." I released her arm, rocked back on my heels and stood.

The blonde drew herself up to her hands and knees, and slowly pushed to her feet. "You're gonna be sorry you did this," she hissed.

"You threatening me?" I made a feint toward her and she flinched back. "Run," I said quietly. "Before I change my mind and kick your ass up and down the street."

She took off and ran after her friends. With a sigh, I brushed off my hands and took Brooke inside the shop.

Brooke's eyes were huge in her face. "What

was that thing you did to her?"

"That was an arm bar hold," I said, and went to pick up the store phone. I hated cops, but I needed to report the incident to be on the safe side. Using the emergency contact list next to the phone, I dialed the Sherriff's department.

After speaking to the dispatch who was sending out a deputy to take a report, I hung up the phone and discovered that Brooke was staring at me like I'd grown two heads. She was very pale and her blue eyes were enormous. "You're not going to keel over on me—are you?"

"She didn't hit me that hard," Brooke said.

"Does it hurt?" When she didn't answer me right away, I steered her over to one of the stools behind the counter. "Sit down," I said.

Brooke dropped to the stool. "What was that? That thing you did to Clementine out there?"

"It's called a controlled force take down," I said, leaning closer to look for an injury. "It's not meant to hurt—but to get control of someone."

"Where did you learn to do that?" Her voice

was awed.

Amused, I lifted her chin and tilted her face toward the light. "I told you I worked security for a while, but I mainly worked as a bartender, and I broke up my share of fights."

"You broke up fights in a bar?" Brooke's eyes were huge.

"Only if I had no other choice."

"Did it happen a lot?" Brooke sounded half-curious—half thrilled.

Satisfied that she was okay, I let go of her face. "With the dancers at the strip club...Yeah, it did. Tempers ran high and bitches fight dirty."

"Wow," Brooke said. "Like cat fights?"

I nodded. "Hair pulling, scratching, biting…I learned fast to put someone in a controlled hold, until they could calm down."

"That was totally cool," Brooke said. "Will you teach me how to do that arm hold thingy?"

I pursed my lips and considered the girl. "It'd be better teaching you some basic self-defense."

"I asked Garrett last year," Brooke said. "But he said I should avoid getting into fights."

I rolled my eyes. "Well, that's all fine and

good but it's never a bad thing for a woman to know how to protect herself, or someone else."

"Who taught you?" Brooke wanted to know.

I smiled. "My mother did. She was a Major in the Air Force and she was smart, tough and strong."

The tan Sherriff's car pulled up and parked at the curb in front of the shop. Brooke reached out and grasped my hand. "Am I going to be in trouble?"

"Of course not," I said. "Camilla does have security cameras and they probably caught the whole thing."

"Oh shit," Brooke whispered, as she watched the deputy exit his car and start for the shop. "Garrett and Dru are going to be so mad at me."

"No, they won't," I said. "Those girls ganged up on you. You did nothing wrong."

"At least I didn't end up in the ER with a broken arm this time."

Brooke's words had me sucking in a deep breath. "You ended up in the hospital last time?"

"Yeah," Brooke said miserably. "Got a hell of a shiner, too. That's what Dru called it—a shiner."

"I see," I managed to say, even while the thought of her having her arm broken made me furious, it also made me wish that I'd have put more pressure on Clementine's arm when I'd had her pinned. I reminded myself to stay calm. "You've tangled with Clementine and her gang before?"

"Yeah," Brooke mumbled, staring at the floor.

"Make sure you tell the cops that."

"Okay," Brooke whispered as the door opened.

The deputy's name was Zak Parker, and we lucked out. He was young, friendly and sympathetic. He viewed the security camera video and grinned when he watched me subdue the blonde teenage bully. He asked Brooke if she was all right, and Brooke admitted that she'd had an altercation—she actually used that word. An 'altercation' with Clementine Bryant a year before at school.

As I listened to Brooke explain that the blonde had been suspended for the previous school fight, I began to understand the comments the girls had made about Brooke changing schools. Deputy Parker promised to notify the private school's safety officer and passed me his card.

He used his cell phone to take a recording of the video surveillance, and while he was in the backroom, I took Brooke out to the sales floor.

"Take a deep breath," I advised her. "Remember, you did nothing wrong. It's going to be okay."

Nervously, she clung to my hand. "Do you really think so?"

"*Claro que si*—of course," I translated when she'd frowned in confusion. I took a deep breath and tried to project some confidence to the girl. "Now, why don't we—"

"Oh, no," Brooke said, staring in horror over my shoulder.

I swung around to see what had upset her, and to my surprise, Chauncey and Philippe Marquette came bursting into the store.

CHAPTER SEVEN

"Camilla!" they called out.

Philippe zeroed in on Brooke. "What happened?"

"Whoa, whoa." I waved them off. "Calm down guys."

Chauncey walked directly to me. "I saw the Sherriff's car out front. Were you robbed?"

"No. We weren't," I said. "Deputy Parker is in the back room looking at the security tapes."

"Why?" Philippe demanded.

"Brooke ran into a bit of trouble on her way home," I began. "There was an...altercation," I used Brooke's word, it seemed to fit the situation perfectly. "And I stepped in."

"Brooke." Philippe put an arm around the girl's shoulders. "You promised. No more fighting."

"I didn't start it!" she whispered furiously.

"It was four against one," I said, calmly.

Aghast, Philippe turned to stare at me. "What happened?"

Brooke pointed a shaky finger at me. "Estella jumped in and did this thing to Clementine. It put her face down on the sidewalk!"

Chauncey's mouth dropped open. "You did *what*?"

I shrugged. "It was nothing."

Deputy Parker stepped out of the back room, and our conversation came to a screeching halt. "That ought to do it," he said with a smile.

"Thank you, Deputy," I said politely.

"If you have any more problems, you have my number. Don't hesitate to call."

"I will," I said, even though I had no intention of doing so.

The deputy nodded toward the girl. "Brooke, with your guardian out of town, maybe you should have someone pick you up from school for a few days and avoid walking home the same route."

"Yes, sir," she said meekly.

“I’ll pick her up myself,” Philippe spoke up.

“Good.” Deputy Parker nodded. “I’ll go speak to Clementine’s parents. Once they see their daughter’s behavior for themselves, I don’t think you’ll have any more problems.” He smiled and let himself out.

As soon as the deputy left the store both Philippe and Chauncey wanted details. To save time and dramatics, I took them in the back and had them watch the security footage.

“That was so *cool*,” Brooke said after it was finished.

Philippe and Chauncey had both shifted to stare at me.

“What?” I asked.

Chauncey grinned. “You are a woman of hidden talents, Estella.”

“Oh, for god’s sake.” I heaved an exasperated sigh. “It wasn’t a big deal. I’ve dealt with much worse when I tended bar—”

“She broke up fights at a strip club too!” Brooke said proudly, causing both men to stare at the girl.

“You worked at a strip club?” Chauncey’s lips twitched.

I scowled at him. "Take that stupid look off your face. I worked as security for the dancers. I was *not* the entertainment."

"Security?" Philippe repeated.

I folded my arms over my chest. "No one ever suspects a woman to be the security detail keeping the customers out of the dressing rooms and away from the dancers." I shrugged. "It paid extremely well."

Philippe did a double take. "I'm sure it did."

"Honestly," I said, "I broke up more catfights between the exotic dancers, and the drag queens, than I did dealing with the customers."

"Yeah," Brooke nodded, solemnly. "Because bitches fight dirty."

I kept a straight face at the men's shocked reaction to Brooke's words. "That's a fact." I nodded to the girl.

"Estella is going to teach me self-defense!" Brooke announced.

Philippe started to laugh and turned it into a cough. "I see."

I folded my arms across my chest. "You got a problem with that?"

"No." He smiled. "Not at all."

When Cammy came back from the post office, Philippe and Chauncey were still at the store. The inevitable retelling of the tale and my newfound hero status, courtesy of Brooke, made me pretty uncomfortable. Plus, I was steaming mad now that I knew the history behind the bullying.

Needing a break from the family's reaction to the news, I announced that I was taking a fifteen-minute break. Giving them a friendly wave, I strolled out of the store and went to clear my head. I walked down the main road, past the small library, and headed to the parking area off the highway that allowed folks to view the river.

The wind whipped my hair back from my face, and I tucked my hands in the pockets of my jeans and stood, taking in the view. I'd managed maybe five minutes of solitude when I heard gravel crunching behind me. I shot a glance over my shoulder and discovered that Chauncey was walking toward me.

"I wanted to check on you to see how you were doing," he said.

Offended, I glared. "*Ay dios mio*! Do I seem

like the kind of person that would be emotionally distraught over breaking up a fight?"

"You seemed upset," Chauncey said, stepping beside me.

"I'm pissed, knowing that those middle school bitches beat Brooke up and broke her arm last year."

Chauncey made a noise of agreement.

"If I'd have known *that* I'd have used a hell of a lot more force on that blonde," I admitted.

"Philippe and Gabriella both told me about what happened to Brooke," he said. "I do know that is one of the reasons Garrett agreed she could go to a public school this year."

"I'm glad she's out of there, then." I nodded.

"As far as I know, she's happier at her new school," Chauncey said quietly. Mimicking my pose, he tucked his hands in his pockets and stood with me, watching the river across the road.

We stood in companionable silence, looking out over the water for a while. "There's something about this place," I finally said. "It's only a little riverside village, in the middle of nowhere, but for some reason it tugs at me." I rotated slightly and took in the curvy limestone cliffs. "Sometimes, depending on the light, it gives me chills. Makes me wonder why it seems so damn familiar."

"Were you ever here before?" Chauncey asked.

"Nope." I shrugged. "My father died when I was almost five and my mother never brought me here...unless this is all like a hereditary memory, or something."

"The first time I saw this place I'd thought my brother had lost his mind choosing to settle here and fix up the old family vineyards and the mansion."

"Doesn't that big gothic house creep you out?"

"It looks amazingly different since Philippe started working on it a couple of years ago. Have Gabriella show you pictures of the renovations some time."

"But what about your own family history? Knowing you had an ancestor who...well, let's say was *suspected* of bumping off his wife?"

"We don't know what happened." Chauncey

shrugged. "It would be fair to say, however, that I don't care for his portrait."

"I'll bet not, it looks a lot like you," I said. "A younger, longer-haired version of you."

"I am several years older than he was." Chauncey pointed out.

"How old are you?"

"Twenty-nine. Pierre-Michel only lived to be twenty-four."

"Yeah, you're ancient by comparison." I squinted over at him. "Plus, you've got the man-scruff thing going on."

Chauncey raised his brows. "Man-scruff?"

"Yeah, the sort of super-short beard that some guys do. You can pull it off with your darker facial hair. Looks good on you."

"Well, thank you." He seemed surprised, maybe even pleased.

"It wasn't a compliment—shit, I'm *not* flirting with you. I was just saying, compared to Pierre-Michel. You know, you have the facial hair..." I trailed off, slightly embarrassed at the way he was studying me.

I told myself to shut up before I said anything else stupid and watched as a flock of gulls gathered over the river.

"I do understand what you mean about the landscape feeling familiar, though." Chauncey said. "There are times when I too, get the oddest feeling that I've been here before."

"Like déjà vu?"

He nodded. "Parts of the house affect me like that too. When Philippe first gave me a tour of the third-floor, I had these memories of the house. But that's not possible, because up until this summer, I'd never been here before."

I watched him as he spoke. *So, I wasn't the only one having weird out-of-place memories,* I thought. I wasn't sure if that was comforting or not.

"Are you ready to go back?" he asked.

I took in a deep breath, blew it out slowly, and nodded. "Yeah, I'm calmer now. I didn't figure it would do Brooke any good to see me lose my temper."

As I started back, Chauncey fell in step with me. "After watching what you can do," he said, "I wouldn't want to see you lose your temper either."

"It's easy to subdue a pre-teen girl," I said.

"It's the pissed-off drag queens that are really a challenge."

"You've definitely led a colorful life, Estella," Chauncey said.

I slid my eyes his way. "Well it wasn't jet-setting all over Europe, but it did have its perks."

"Such as?"

"Makeup tips," I said as Chauncey began to grin. "Ain't nobody better at teaching you how to use makeup than a drag queen."

He threw back his head and laughed, and I found myself smiling at the sound of it. Companionably, we walked back to the store.

***

The rest of the week passed without incident. Dru and Garrett were due home from their honeymoon on Sunday afternoon, and apparently I'd earned mad street cred with Brooke. Since the afternoon I'd stepped into that fight, she started following me around, *everywhere*. After being on my own for years, it took some getting used to.

If I was working at the shop, she'd have Philippe drop her off after school so she could hang out. When I was at the farmhouse, she was my own personal shadow. If I studied the books on herbalism, she sat next to me, took notes as well, and shared the basic magick lessons Drusilla had been teaching her.

It was sort of lowering to realize that a twelve-year-old knew more about magick than I did. Maybe it made Brooke happy to be able to teach someone else. Either way, she was now more accepting of my new place within the family.

I volunteered to make dinner Saturday night, *arroz con pollo* with rice, black beans and avocado. Of course, Brooke offered to help me. Which only made it take twice as long as it normally would have.

I cooked the chicken in Priscilla's huge cast iron skillet and listened as the kid chattered up a streak—the entire time.

"Billy Jones in my science class, he sits next to me. And he asked me to be his lab partner."

"That's cool." The chicken was done, so I added onions and peppers to the skillet. While they cooked, I listened to her big adventures in science, and her other classes. Meaning, I now knew more about the social structure of her middle school than I ever wanted to.

At my directions, she handed me the tomatoes, broth and the rice. I mixed those in and waited for it all to come to a boil. I had her working on rinsing the black beans and adding them to a separate pot to heat up.

She stirred the beans and let out a long sigh. I snuck a peek at her and saw that she was blushing. “Is Billy cute?” I asked.

Brooke shrugged, but her face went a brighter shade of red. “Uh, I guess so.”

I turned the skillet down to a simmer and covered it, setting the timer for twenty minutes. “You’re blushing, *mi Rosita*.”

She scrunched up her face in confusion. “*Mi Rosita*? What’s that mean?”

I handed her the avocados to dice up. “Basically, I called you ‘little red’.”

“Oh.” Brooke smiled shyly. “I kinda like that.”

Priscilla walked into the kitchen carrying the baby. Philippe and Gabriella were out at the movies having a date night, and my grandmother was thrilled to babysit.

"It smells amazing in here," Priscilla said, taking a seat at the table. She slipped Danielle in the old wooden high chair. The baby was excited by the voices and noise in the kitchen and started to bang her hands on the tray.

"Fifteen minutes," I predicted, while Brooke set the dicing aside and raced around fetching the baby food for Priscilla. Since Cammy was out with Jacob, it was only the three of us—four, if you counted Danielle.

Calmly, Priscilla began feeding the baby while I pulled the dinner together. I added the shredded cheddar cheese to the skillet and allowed it to begin melting. I scooped the beans in a bowl and placed them on the table. Brooke added her bowl of diced avocados, and I put a folded towel on the table to protect it from the heat before I added the skillet to the center of the table.

I dished up the food and passed it around. I'd barely sat my butt in the chair before there was a knock on the back door.

"Come in, Chauncey!" Priscilla called out.

I swung my head around to stare at my grandmother. She'd known who it was. *Without being able to see who was at the door,* I noted. "Creepy," I muttered.

"She does that," Brooke confided in a low whisper.

Sure enough, Chauncey Marquette poked his head in. "I'm sorry," he said. "Am I interrupting your dinner?"

Priscilla smiled. "Of course not. Why don't you join us? There's plenty. Isn't there, Estella?"

"Sure." I said. "Do you like *arroz con pollo?"*

"Sounds great to me."

I nodded. "Okay sit down, and I'll get you a plate."

"I'll get him some water," Brooke said, and popped back up to do so.

I grabbed a plate and cutlery, and Chauncey sat down in the empty place to my right. I dished up the food, and Brooke passed the beans and avocados.

Priscilla chatted with Chauncey as we dug in, and I wondered at him showing up at dinnertime. He'd never dropped by before. Perhaps she'd invited him...but why?

I watched as my grandmother sampled the food, and when she smiled, I felt my shoulders drop. "This is wonderful," she said.

"Glad you like it." I smiled back.

To my left, the baby banged her hands on her high chair tray.

"Is she still hungry?" Brooke wanted to know.

I took a piece of avocado and smashed it on my plate. I took her baby spoon and scooped some up. "Danielle." I called her name and she turned her head to look at me. I held out the spoon and she opened her mouth. I gave her some, and waited to see how she would react.

I had never watched a baby try a new food for the first time. It was hysterical the way her tiny face scrunched up in concentration. When she smiled and started making happy sounds, I gave her some more.

"She likes it!" Brooke grinned at the baby opening her mouth and leaning forward for more avocado.

"Of course she does." I grinned as the baby

began to babble. "Don't you, *mija*?"

"What does *mija* mean?" Brooke asked me.

"It's like saying 'sweetheart'."

"Oh, sort of like when Philippe calls me *cherie*." Brooke nodded. "I didn't know babies could eat avocados," she said.

"Avocados are very healthy, and mild enough for a six-month-old," Priscilla said to Brooke.

While we ate dinner, Chauncey told us about how the suites were finished at the mansion. "The clean-up crew starts this week."

"Excellent," Priscilla said, and added more avocados to her meal. "That means Gabriella can start with the decorating."

***

After supper, Priscilla volunteered to clean up since I had cooked and Brooke went and sat on the rug in the living room, entertaining the baby. Chauncey and I were shooed out to the gardens and told to enjoy the evening air.

I noticed as we traveled along the shade gardens that he was walking very carefully, and that his leg was dragging a bit. "Did you hurt your leg?" I asked. "Sometimes, I notice that you limp."

Chauncey grimaced. "I was hurt in a racing accident a year and a half ago."

"Racing accident?" I asked. "What type of racing?"

"Cars," he said, staring off into space.

I'd half expected him to say horses. He seemed like the upper crust Brit who would be riding in the forest in one of those riding outfits...*Jodhpurs? Breeches?* Note to self: Look up what they called those types of pants.

I returned my focus on the conversation. "What kind of cars did you race?"

"Formula One."

"Seriously? Like Grand prix stuff?"

He nodded. "Yes."

"You weren't kidding when you said you'd traveled around Europe for your job."

He sighed. "Yes, I was semi-pro, about to move up to the pros, but an accident ended my career." He still hadn't looked at me and was apparently lost in his thoughts.

"I'm sorry," I said, contritely. "I didn't mean to bring up bad memories."

He shifted his head slightly and met my eyes. “You didn’t.”

“How in the hell did you end up in the Midwest?”

“After the accident, when I found out I wouldn’t be able to return to racing, it was a tough time. I had months of physical therapy. I lost my sponsors, my endorsement deals...”

“Don’t tell me. Let me guess,” I said, “and the parties, women, and fancy racing friends you’d had all but disappeared, too.”

He tipped his head to one side and studied me. “That would be correct.”

I tried to sound sympathetic. “Man, that’s tough.”

One side of his mouth quirked up. “I had some money put aside and after I recovered, I started looking for a good investment. Some place new, and with something that would be mine. When my grandfather suggested investing in the winery and old family estate, I flew out here and talked it over with Philippe and Garrett.”

“You’re a world away from the high life and the racing circuit these days.”

He folded his arms across his chest. “I prefer it that way.”

Well, that explained why he’d schmoozed so effortlessly at the wedding reception. “I want a beer,” I said. “Why don’t you take a load off, sit on the bench and I’ll be back in a sec with a couple.”

“That’d be nice.” He sat and stretched out his leg.

I went back inside, snagged a couple of bottles out of the fridge, and twisted off the tops. I was moving to the back door when Priscilla stopped me.

“Are you getting a chance to become better acquainted with Chauncey?”

“Uh, yeah.” I frowned. “Sure. We’re just talking.”

Priscilla’s mouth bowed up. “It’s a pretty night to sit and watch the stars come out.”

“I guess,” I said, pushing open the screen door. I thought about her comment as I hopped down the steps and walked over to Chauncey, who was relaxing on the big chunky blue bench. I held out a bottle to him. “Here you go.”

"Thanks." He took the bottle and I sat beside him.

I tapped my bottle against his and studied the back of the house. I could see my grandmother finishing the clean-up through the windows. She bustled around, and now that I thought about it...She'd been way too innocent with that comment about 'sitting under the stars'. "Tell me Chauncey," I began, "do you drop by often for supper?"

"Not by myself, no. Priscilla called and invited me today. I guess she thinks I'm lonely." Chauncey took a pull on his beer. "Either that, or you grandmother is playing matchmaker."

I promptly choked on my drink. His casual words had caused the beer to stick in my throat while I'd been in mid-swallow. "Oh for god's sake!" I coughed and patted my chest hoping it would go down the right pipe. "She wouldn't try and match us up, would she?"

Chauncey started to grin as I wheezed. "It's sweet of her, if you ask me."

"Sweet?"

"Well, we barely know each other,"

Chauncey chuckled. "Laugh it off, Estella. I am." He leaned back on the bench, giving me a friendly smile.

My back went up. *Laugh it off?* I thought. With an effort, I reconsidered my words and sent him—what I hoped—was a casual smile in return. "Sure, it's all one big joke. After all, I'm a Latina bartender from California—a nobody, and you're the hot-shot ex-racer from Europe. Us together would be pretty funny."

"Exactly," he said, giving me a friendly pat on the shoulder. "I'm sure Priscilla meant well."

The asshole actually thought I wasn't good enough for him. I sat there so simmering mad that it took me a moment to realize that he was still speaking.

"—couple of weeks the open house reception for the suites is being held, you should come."

I shrugged. "Maybe."

"Your family will all be there. You're expected to attend the event as well."

"Why?" I asked. "Did you need a good bartender?"

That snarky comment made him roar with

laughter.

The fact that he found it so freaking hilarious had my temper slipping even further. I took a deep breath in through my nose while Chauncey about bust a gut, laughing over it all.

"I like you," he said, giving me a friendly pat on the shoulder. "I haven't relaxed and laughed this much in a long time."

"Happy to serve." I forced a smile to stay on my face. "That's bartender humor."

He grinned at that. "I should probably get going," he said.

"Okay," was the safest thing I could say in response.

He stood and handed me his half-empty beer. "Tell Priscilla thanks for inviting me for dinner."

"Of course," I said, taking the bottle automatically—like the hired help.

"The food was great." He smiled, and I had to fight the overwhelming urge to toss the bottle at his head.

"I'll be sure and pass your compliments on to the kitchen staff," I said, straight faced.

He thought that was hilarious too, and

wished me a good night. With a wave, Chauncey walked off to his fancy low-slung sports car parked in the back driveway.

I stood there, amazed at the sheer depth of his arrogance, as he backed out of the drive, gave a quick *beep-beep* of his horn, and drove away.

It took me a few minutes to understand that the emotion I was feeling wasn't merely anger. It was hurt. I was hurt by his dismissal of me, *and* his attitude.

Deliberately, I walked to the recycle bins at the top of the driveway and dropped the bottles inside. I let the lid slam closed and stalked back toward the house. "You think you're better than me Chauncey Marquette?" I muttered. "Because you were a famous racer in Europe?" I stomped up the back steps and sat on the back porch.

Was the guy an aristocrat or something? Was that why he acted so casually superior? *And by the way,* I thought. *You're in the states now, baby. A title don't mean shit here.*

I pulled out my cell, opened my internet browser and started to see what I could find online about Chauncey Marquette *and* his past.

CHAPTER EIGHT

I found out a lot, actually. There was article after article posted about Chauncey's rise to the top of his field, background in English society, and racing career. There was quite a bit on his crash—bad ones in Formula One cars weren't as common as they used to be, according to the articles I read online.

I found several more posts about his forced retirement from the sport. On a hunch, I hit social media and my jaw dropped at the sheer number of photos of the man with different beautiful women, from every rich playground in the world I'd ever heard of.

Monte Carlo, the French Riviera, Lake Como, Milan, I lost count of the tropical islands he and his 'friends' had taken selfies on. It only made it more curious to me, as to why he'd ultimately settled here. In the middle of nowhere small historic village, along the river in Illinois.

I shifted my search to his injuries and recovery, and that's when I found an older article from some British tabloid. They'd managed to get a picture of Chauncey wearing a leg brace and using a walker. He was with an older gentleman with flowing silver hair, and the caption noted that the photo had been taken outside of a physical rehab facility. Chauncey had worn a ball cap and shades, but you could still tell it was him. He was thinner and pale, but it was definitely him.

I went back to social media again and checked his 'friends' accounts, looking to see if any of them had included him in their posts *after* his accident. They hadn't. In fact, they'd apparently continued with their partying and race-circuit travel, forever in search of the perfect Instagram photo, and trying to outdo each other in competition for the most 'likes'.

Currently, Chauncey didn't appear to have any social media accounts, which made me wonder if he'd deleted all of them. My gut said he had.

I clicked off my internet browser and thought over everything I knew about him. He was used to the finer things. The best schools, travel, and when he'd been in the sport, lots of cash and supermodels.

The man used to be rich and famous...and now he was living quietly and, for all intents and purposes, anonymously. I wonder if he missed it all. I thought back to what he'd said to me the night of the wedding about his luck running out.

Maybe it had.

***

Dru and Garrett returned from their honeymoon, and Brooke went back home. After a week of her being at the farmhouse, I sort of missed her. Cammy began to show me how to make different kinds of soaps in the evenings, cold press she called it. And I helped her make some seasonal Halloween varieties of soap too.

I spent the next few weeks working at the boutique with Cammy, and the month of

October began. Just as Dru had said, the color in the trees began to put on a hell of a show. I helped Cammy decorate the shop for Halloween, and when I got my first paycheck, I cashed it and headed straight for the closest mall.

I was determined to find a few more things to wear besides the jeans, two cotton blouses, a hoodie, and the slogan t-shirts I'd brought from California. Bottom line, the stuff I had wasn't nice enough to keep wearing to work every day and, well…I would need clothes for cooler weather now that autumn had set in.

Almost right away, I found a red long sleeve dress in the wrap-around style. Standing in the fitting room, I debated over it. I'd need something to wear to the opening of the hotel suites at the Marquette mansion. I didn't want to wear the sequined dress again so soon after Dru's wedding. Determinedly, I eyeballed the two sweaters and black dress pants I had also planned to purchase.

"New life, new wardrobe," I told myself.

I changed back into my own clothes, scooped up all the garments I'd been considering, and marched toward the check-out counter with the grim resolve of a woman going into battle. I was about to spend every penny I'd just made on clothes.

"What a pretty dress." The sales clerk smiled. "I bet that red looks great on you."

"Uh, thanks." I felt a bead of sweat run down my back and hoped I had enough cash on me to cover the purchases—otherwise I'd have to put something back.

"Do you have any sales coupons?"

I shook my head. "No, I don't."

"That's okay." The sales clerk pulled a stack of flyers out from under the counter. "I have extra."

With the help of the coupons, I had enough to buy the dress, sweaters, and the slacks. The sales clerk did her coupon mojo and got the dress to discount thirty percent, and the sweaters were buy one get one half price. I smiled at her kindness. "Wow, thank you very much."

She bagged everything for me, and I walked away with fifty bucks still in my wallet. I headed for the discount shoe store I'd spotted and decided to hit up their clearance racks to see if I could luck out and find a pair of black heels that actually fit.

I did, and they were discounted at eighty percent off too. I was leaving the shoe place when I saw a national chain store that specialized in casual clothes. I was, in all likelihood, kind of high on my bargain shoe purchase, but before I could talk myself out of it, I ducked in the store. I bought myself two long-sleeved shirts, one in a chili pepper red, and the other in black. I picked up a pair of inexpensive plaid flannel pajama bottoms too. The nights were already getting cooler.

As I stood in the check-out line, I spotted a glittery star pendant on a long gold-tone chain. It had been marked down to $2.99, so I added it to my purchases. While the practical long-sleeved scoop neck t-shirts weren't fancy, they *were* on sale, and they'd certainly brighten up my jeans. Plus, the sparkly pendant would pop against the red dress I'd purchased.

I drove back to the farmhouse, enjoying the scenery and taking in the changing leaves on the trees along the river road. The October sunshine was bright, and I was totally fascinated by the color in the trees. They changed more every day. It was like magick. I sang along with the radio, happier than I'd been in a long time. I'd barely made it in the front door when Cammy pounced.

"Oooh, shopping adventure!" She rubbed her hands together. "What did you get?"

"A couple of things…" I said, heading up the stairs to my room.

Cammy followed me in and started poking through the bags as soon as I dropped them on the bench at the foot of the bed. "Wow, nice sweaters!" She held the burnt orange one up. "Now that it's getting cooler, you can wear this to work at the shop."

"That was the plan." I walked over to my closet and retrieved a hanger for the dress. "I can't keep wearing *Lotions & Potions* t-shirts every day."

"It wouldn't hurt you to dress up a bit more," Cammy agreed.

"Yeah well, I had to wait until I got paid to get a few new things." I slipped the red dress out of the bag and hung it up.

Cammy pulled the long-sleeved t-shirts out of the bag. "I noticed you never shipped any of your other belongings here."

"There was nothing to ship. I brought everything I had with me."

Cammy's eyes were huge. "Every piece of clothing you owned fit in that duffle bag?"

I shrugged. "I know how to pack. My mom was military, remember?"

She placed the sparkly star pendant on top of the stack of t-shirts before she spoke. "I was afraid that you hadn't shipped the rest of your belongings here because you weren't sure whether or not you were staying."

Surprised, I tipped my head to one side. "Where else would I go? There's nothing left for me in California. I sold whatever things I had—and there wasn't much—before I came out here."

"I had no idea." Cammy's voice was quiet.

I pulled out my dress shoes from the plastic shopping bag and tucked them in the shoebox on the empty closet shelf. I turned around to face her. "I didn't—and don't—want Priscilla to know, the uh, circumstances, that I'd been in before she found me."

"Were you in trouble?"

"I'd been fired from my job, my car had up and died, and I was late on the rent." Worrying over the back rent was keeping me up at night, but I didn't want Cammy to know that. I went over and picked up the new pendant, silently telling myself that I could start chipping away at that debt with my next paycheck.

"You left at night, and got out quick, didn't you?"

I frowned. "You doing that psychic shit again?"

Cammy tapped a finger to her temple. "This picture of you getting on a bus at night popped into my head."

"Good guess.'

"I didn't guess."

I chuckled. "Well it's a safe bet that a limo is way out of my price range, *chica*."

Cammy folded her hands in her lap. "Do you need any help now, financially?"

I stared at her. "I'm sure as hell not asking you for a loan."

Cammy stood and walked over to the dresser,

carrying the two sweaters. “Let me put these away for you.” She opened the top drawer, hesitated, and slid open the second. She shut them both. Cammy opened the third drawer, then blew out a long breath. “I feel like such an ass.”

“Why?” I asked.

“I owe you an apology,” Cammy said. “I’ve been giving you grief for the past couple of weeks about wearing something other than store t-shirts to work. I didn’t realize you’d been doing that because you didn’t have anything else to wear.”

I fought not to let my embarrassment show. “Well, I have a few more things now, so no worries.” Gently, I folded the dress pants over a hanger and added them to the closet. Now, five things hung in there. My old denim jacket, the black dress I’d borrowed from Cammy, the navy sequined one I’d worn to Dru’s wedding, my new slacks, and the red dress I’d just purchased. A tiny thrill went through me. It was nice to see pretty clothes hanging inside my closet.

“You should have told me,” Cammy said.

"Told you what?" I asked, closing the closet door. "That all I owned was jeans, a couple of old button-down cotton blouses, and a handful of slogan tees? When I admitted that I didn't have anything appropriate to wear to Dru's wedding, that wasn't a play for sympathy. I didn't have anything."

"Still." Cammy frowned. "I wish you'd have confided in me."

"Confided what?" I snapped at her. "That I was too broke to buy any new clothes?"

"I would have taken you shopping." Cammy rested her hand on my arm. "Gotten you some basics. Whatever you needed."

"You already gave me a job. That was enough. I'm not a charity case, Camilla!"

Cammy tossed her head. "I never said you were, and I offered you the job because *I* needed the help!" Her voice went up and, oddly, the light on the dresser started to flicker. "I was only stating that I'd have helped you, Estella—*if* I had known."

"Girls!" Priscilla poked her head in the door. "What's with all the shouting?"

"I'm sorry," I apologized immediately. "We

were arguing. I shouldn't have raised my voice in your home."

Priscilla narrowed her eyes. "It's your home as well, young lady."

"Apparently, Estella doesn't feel like this is her home!" Cammy said, hotly, and the light bulb in the lamp popped and went out.

I flinched away from the loud noise, then studied Cammy as she stood there, seething mad. "I don't get why you're all bent out of shape."

"I suppose," she said through her teeth, "I figured after three weeks of you living here, and working with me, that you'd trust me a little more,"

"I don't give my trust easily," I said flatly. "Don't take it personally."

"But we're sisters," Cammy argued.

"Biologically, we are," I agreed.

She pressed a hand against her heart. "And do you have any feelings towards your biological family?"

"I've been on my own a long time, Camilla. The family thing is new to me, and I'm trying to figure all this out as I go."

"I see." Cammy nodded. "You don't trust anyone and you are a loner. Yet you didn't seem to have any problems standing up for Brooke a couple weeks ago."

"Of course I would help her. She's only a kid!" I planted my hands on my hips. "Do you have any idea what it's like out there in the real world—outside of Ames Crossing? Jesus, it's cruel, ugly and hard. I've seen enough to last a lifetime. I will *never* stand by and watch someone be abused or bullied. It's simply not who I am."

"Well said, Estella," Priscilla cut in. "Your father was very much the same. It was one of the reasons he joined the military."

Cammy folded her arms defensively across her chest. "I apologize if I pushed too hard, or too fast. For me, when I first saw you at the airport, that was it. You are my sister and I love you. I only wanted to help, Estella. I'm sorry you're not ready to accept that."

Her words made me feel ungracious, which I'd bet was exactly the reason she'd said them. I took a deep breath and chose my next words with care. "I'm very grateful for the job,

Cammy, and for everything you've been teaching me. I'm sorry if I hurt your feelings."

"Perhaps," Priscilla said, "you need to be more patient, Cammy, and give Estella some time."

"I'll try." Cammy shrugged. "I'm simply not a patient person by nature."

"There's a shocker." I rolled my eyes. "Look, I'm not used to being around so many girly females. There hasn't been much opportunity in my life to embrace my softer side. So maybe you could cut me some slack."

Cammy blew out a long breath. "Meaning?"

I raised my eyebrows. "I'm tough. I've had to be."

Cammy tipped her head toward the dresser. "Hence the *Bad-ass Bitch* t-shirt I saw in your top drawer."

"It suits me."

Cammy snorted out a laugh. "I watched the security video of how you handled that mean-girl. Trust me, I *believe* you."

"Young Brooke has been singing your praises since that day," Priscilla said.

I sighed. "Yeah, I know."

"Are we done arguing now, ladies?" Priscilla asked brightly.

I blew out a breath. "I sure as hell hope so."

"Wonderful." My grandmother smiled. "I feel like going out for dinner tonight. My treat."

Cammy smiled. "Where did you want to go, Gran?"

Priscilla patted her hair. "I want a burger, something greasy and horribly unhealthy."

"I suppose I could wear one of my new shirts," I said.

"I like this red one," my grandmother said as she pointed out the shirt still folded on the bed.

"Okay, gimme a second to change and we can go."

Priscilla drove us into Alton, and I got the shock of my life when she pulled up to what was clearly a biker hangout. She and Cammy strolled inside and, intrigued, I followed. I got another shock when I saw families sitting in booths and tables as well. The place was a dive, but also a tourist trap all rolled into one. The food however, smelled great.

I sat back in my chair at the table after we ordered and let out a long sigh. For the first time since leaving Bakersfield, I felt at home.

***

I had wondered if the party to celebrate the grand opening of the suites at the Marquette mansion would be upscale, and as soon as I walked into the manor house that night, I could see that it was. The decorations were fancy autumnal and *gilded*, I supposed was the right word. Everything seemed to glimmer with metallic accents. Seemed like anybody who thought they were important had showed up to the mansion that night and were ready to party.

I knew from hearing the family talk about it that Nicole Dubois, the PR manager for the winery, had used the opening of the suites as a way to link the winery and the event venues together. And as I walked around with my glass of wine, I realized she'd been damn clever to do so.

Drusilla moved over to me with a smile on her face. "Estella! I love that red dress!"

I accepted the kiss on the cheek, simply because there was no way to dodge it. "Thanks,

Dru." I smiled. "It's new."

"I wish I could pull off that bright of a color," Dru sighed. "Never works on me."

I eyeballed her lacy mauve dress. "And I can't pull off pastels...so it all balances out. How's Brooke doing?" I asked.

"She's at home with Mrs. Huntley, our housekeeper."

"Well, that's probably for the best," I agreed.

Dru nodded. "She's sulking a bit because she couldn't be here tonight. After all, she's technically a part of the original *Trois Amis*."

"Shouldn't they be four friends? I asked. "Now that Chauncey has invested in the winery, event venue, and the hotel?"

Drusilla chuckled. "They'd never rename it. Besides, Chauncey prefers working mostly behind the scenes these days."

"Oh, is he here tonight?" I tried to sound casual.

"Of course." Dru smiled. "He's so proud of the renovations to the western wing of the mansion. As well he should be. If it wasn't for him, we'd never been able to move onto stage three of the business plan so soon."

"Stage three?" I asked.

Dru accepted a glass of wine from a passing waiter. "Sure, stage one was to get the winery going and open." She sipped her wine. "Stage two was to turn the first floor of the western wing of the house, and the terraces, into event venue spaces..."

"Which would help cover the cost of the renovations," I said with a nod.

Dru nodded. "And it's a smart way to make the house start paying for itself."

"Yeah, I bet maintaining a house this size, isn't cheap," I agreed. "So what's stage three?"

"Stage three was to turn the second and third western floors into upscale hotel suites. That way wedding parties or brides and grooms could have their event here *and* spend the night."

I smiled. "I'm afraid to ask if there is a stage four."

Dru gave me a friendly elbow nudge. "There is now. We're going to start working on transforming the formal gardens behind the manor into a space suitable for outdoor weddings or events next spring."

"Nice," I said. "I'm going to take a wild guess that you're going to have a hand in that transformation."

"Max and I have been working on landscaping plans that will pay homage to the old formal walled gardens, but with a more cottage garden type of feel."

"Like a secret garden, kind of thing?" I asked.

"Exactly!" Dru said with a broad smile.

"So, you and Gabriella will expand on the wildflowers you planted this year?"

"Right!" Dru practically rubbed her hands together. "I can hardly wait to get started in the spring."

We chatted for a few more moments, and then she left to go and help Garrett with a drawing for some lucky attendee to win a big basket full of cheese, crackers, wine glasses, and *Trois Amis* wines.

The party had been in swing for an hour, and folks were hitting the open bar—and the free wine—hard. In the background I saw Philippe, Garrett and Nicole standing at an information table, passing out brochures to guests about the new suites, the winery, and of course the event venues.

Chauncey, I'd been informed, was currently taking small groups of guests on a tour of the now complete suites on the second and third floors. Cammy and her fiancé Jacob had chatted me up, and of course, she'd jokingly threatened to take me on a private ghost tour of the third floor. She said she wanted me to see all the 'hot spots'.

I sipped my wine and thought about ways in which I could avoid that. Jacob distracted Cammy and they went to talk to another couple. With a shrug, I decided to wander over toward the bar. There was a single leather-covered stool open, and I snagged it. Sliding across the seat, I started to chat up the bartender.

"Hey, Jaxon." I smiled at the college student I'd met who'd also been working the night of Dru's wedding. "How goes it?"

"Hi ya, Estella." He topped off my wine before I could ask. "It's going."

He and another guy were working as fast as they could. His co-worker was opening bottles of wine, pouring out samples, and explaining the different varieties to the guests.

The conversations buzzed happily around me, and I overheard a few people talking about booking the venue for weddings, or parties. *That'd be great news for Gabriella and Philippe,* I thought. The house was massive, and even with Chauncey investing, I bet the amount of money it had cost to renovate the vineyards and the old house had been mind-blowing.

I sat, swinging a foot at the bar, and sipped my wine. Honestly, I would have preferred a beer. However, this wasn't that type of crowd. The white wine from the *Trois Amis* winery wasn't bad, I decided. Not too dry or sweet, it managed to hit somewhere in the middle.

I wasn't much of a wine drinker, I thought, sliding my new golden star pendant back and forth on its chain. *But maybe I should learn.*

It was more accidental than deliberate when I tuned into the conversation of the well-to-do couple seated next to me at the bar. The man was trying to talk his lady friend into leaving the party. He wasn't keeping his voice down anymore, and he probably thought he was being very smooth. The man was just drunk enough that he was speaking too loudly, and bordering on sloppy.

The woman appeared to be in her early thirties. She was quietly pretty with her dark plum, short-sleeved dress. Her hair was brown and done up in a French twist, she also wore trendy blush-pink glasses. I pegged her for a teacher, maybe a librarian. But at the moment she had her hands full, keeping her date in line.

I caught Jaxon's attention and indicated the couple with a tilt of my head.

"Been keeping an eye on him," Jaxon said as he passed another guest a mixed drink.

The drunk man at the bar called for another round, and he didn't take it well when Jaxon informed him that he'd been cut off. He shifted his aggravation toward his date and tried to get the woman to leave with him, right then.

"I don't think so, Tony." She grimaced. "You're drunk and have embarrassed me enough. I'm leaving."

"I paid a lot for these tickets tonight." Tony's voice was raised. "Where the hell do you think you're going, Amanda?"

Amanda curled her lip. “Anywhere but here.” She managed about two steps away before drunk Tony jumped up from his barstool. His aggressive movement had all my muscles coiling.

He grabbed Amanda by her elbow. “Don’t you walk away from me!”

Now the couple were standing right behind me, and Tony was not only drunk, he was belligerent and mean.

CHAPTER NINE

"I'm giving you a great offer," the man said to his date. "A plain woman like you should be flattered."

"Let go of me!" Amanda tried to pull away.

"That's enough," I said, swiveling around on my barstool. "She said she's not interested."

"Mind your own business," Tony snarled, and tightened his grip on the woman's arm, making her yelp in pain.

"That's not gonna happen." I slid off my barstool. "Now," I said, conversationally, "what *is* going to happen is that you are going to let go of the lady's arm and leave her alone."

The fact that Tony had a good six inches on me in height didn't concern me in the least. I'd learned to stand my ground a long time ago. I could take a soft, spoiled rich man in an expensive suit with a minimum of effort. I'd simply prefer not to make a scene at my family's party.

Tony looked me up and down. "Little girl, do you know who I am?"

I smiled. "Yeah, you're the *pendejo* that's going to walk away, or end up on his ass."

"Stay out of this, bitch!" Tony snarled.

"Estella?" Jaxon's voice sounded worried.

I didn't spare the bartender a glance. Instead, I kept my eyes locked on Tony. "Last warning," I said firmly. "Let go of her. Now."

With an inarticulate roar, Tony shoved his date away. It was a hard enough push that she tumbled backwards. I started to reach for her, but Tony lifted his fist and took a swing at my head. I easily dodged the sloppy punch and a few women screamed even though he missed me by a mile.

There went all my hopes for not making a scene.

"*Hijo de puta*," I hissed, and planted a swift uppercut under Tony's chin.

Tony's eyes rolled back in his head. His

knees gave out and he toppled over, taking a barstool with him as he landed with a crash—on his ass—and on the floor.

People stood there gaping as I reached down and helped the woman stand back up. "Are you okay?" I asked.

Her face was pale. So pale, that I could see freckles dusted across her nose and cheeks. "Yes." She nodded. "Thank you!"

I patted her arm. "Happy to help."

Suddenly Chauncey, Philippe, and Garrett were there. "Estella!" They spoke all at once. "Are you all right?"

"Fine," I said. "You may want to help the lady, though. She's pretty shaken up." I passed her off to Garrett.

Deputy Zak Parker stepped in, and he casually hauled Tony to his feet. "Hello, Estella." He nodded.

"Deputy," I said, with resignation. "I didn't know you were here tonight." I hadn't spotted the deputy, and he too was wearing a suit and tie. Clearly, he'd been off duty.

"You sure do know how to keep things interesting," he said. With a few quiet words to

Philippe, he marched Tony outside.

The woman I'd helped rubbed her arm. "Thank you for the rescue. I had no idea he'd turn into *that*."

I frowned when I saw the red marks from Tony's grip. "Do you need a ride home?" I asked, kindly. "We can call you a cab."

She blew out a long shaky breath. "Yes, I would appreciate that very much."

"Allow me to take care of that for you," Garrett said, gallantly.

She fished in her purse. "Here's my business card." She handed it over, and her pale green eyes seemed to look right into me. "If I can ever help you in anyway, please contact me."

I nodded and skimmed the card. It read: Amanda Beaumont. I also saw she was the branch manager of the local library, and I smiled. "Nice to meet you, Amanda." *Librarian,* I thought, smugly. *Can I call 'em or what?*

"And you are?" she asked.

"Estella. Estella Flores."

She shook my hand and I felt the weirdest little snap of electricity. "Thanks for the save,

Estella."

I nodded. "Sure thing."

Garrett stepped in and escorted Amanda away from the gawkers. The crowd was breaking up, and Chauncey smoothed things over and distracted everyone by announcing they were about to give away a free, one night stay at the suites.

"Please follow Nicole Dubois, our PR manager into the lounge for the drawing." Chauncey's voice sounded unruffled, and sure enough, the looky-loos followed along after Nicole.

I picked up the barstool, set it upright and headed behind the bar. Jaxon gave me a friendly pat on the shoulder as I passed him, and I helped myself to a clean towel, making an icepack for my knuckles. *Damn,* I thought, *I was way out of practice to have them start throbbing so quickly.*

I'd barely finished wrapping the ice in the towel when all my sisters came whipping around the bar.

"Estella!" Gabriella reached me first. "Let me see." She picked up my hand, inspecting my knuckles.

"Holy crap!" Cammy grabbed one of my shoulders. "I saw you take him down from across the room."

"Did you hurt your hand?" Gabriella wanted to know.

I eased my hand away from her, "I'm fine. The ice is to keep my knuckles from swelling."

Dru crossed her arms over her chest. "This isn't the first time you've decked somebody."

"Nope," I said cheerfully. "Probably won't be the last time, either."

"You're not even angry," Gabriella said.

I shrugged. "No, of course not. I am sorry though that the guy made a scene at your grand opening."

"*Pfft.*" Gabriella rolled her eyes. "Don't you worry about that."

Philippe waded in through the women. Silently, he took my right hand, inspecting my knuckles for himself. He shifted his eyes to mine and gently laid the ice-filled towel across them.

I didn't flinch when the ice went over my knuckles, but instead, held his gaze calmly.

"Nice work," he said.

"Thanks," I said. "Is Amanda okay?"

"Garrett is calling a cab for her," Philippe answered.

"She might want to file a complaint against Tony. She's going to have a nasty bruise on her arm from where he grabbed her."

"I believe the deputy will take care of that. Why don't you sit down for a moment?" He tucked his arm around my waist and steered me to a nearby table.

My lips twitched. "Philippe, this is really sweet, but I don't need to sit down." He nudged me into a chair anyway. "I'm fine," I said, starting to rise, and before I got half way out of the chair, the other three chairs at the table were filled by my sisters. Resigned, I sat. "Look, I told you before, I can handle myself."

Cammy leaned forward. "Trust me, after seeing you in action first hand, we all believe you."

Seeing me in action. I winced. "Where's Priscilla?"

"Gran volunteered to give a prospective bride and groom a tour of the terrace area." Drusilla said.

"Lucky for me, then." I smiled.

Philippe patted my head. "Can I get you anything, *harpie*?"

The tone was indulgent, but the word threw me. "What did you just call me?"

"A hell-cat," Gabriella explained. "It's a term of endearment."

"For the Midnight women, at any rate," Philippe said, straight-faced.

I chuckled. Philippe was sort of starting to grow on me. Damned if I knew why.

Jacob walked up and set a full glass of wine in front of me. "Compliments of Jaxon, the bartender."

"Nice," I said, appreciatively.

Jacob grinned at me, even as he rested his hands on Cammy's shoulders. "I figured you earned it."

"My hero," I said. I picked up the glass, toasted the bartender, and my sister's fiancé. Tossing back the wine, I drained the glass, and slapped it back on the table as if I'd done a shot of Patrón.

Cammy raised one eyebrow. "Estella, you are

so hard-core."

Drusilla promptly lost it. She dropped her head into her hands and laughed until she cried.

I waited until she came up for air. "Are you okay, Dru?"

She wiped her eyes. "No wonder Brooke wants you to teach her self defense."

"It's not a bad idea..." I began.

"Oh, I agree." Dru grinned. "But only if you promise to show me a few moves as well."

I winked at her. "Deal." I began to notice people were moving closer to our table. *Trying to eavesdrop,* I figured. I scanned the room and noted that most of the partygoers were now staring directly at me.

Cammy nudged me with her elbow, "Now that the excitement is over, Rocky. How about that private ghost tour of the haunted third floor?"

I waved her off. "Hard pass."

She smirked. "Still afraid of running into the ghosts?"

I rolled my eyes at her. "Of course not."

Cammy leaned back in her chair. "No, I understand. The paranormal realm is frightening for some—"

"I never said that I was scared," I argued.

"Prove it," she said, fluffing the ends of her pink hair. "Let's go poke around on the third floor and see what we can discover."

"Stop teasing her," Gabriella said to Cammy.

"Stop being such a mom." Cammy rolled her eyes.

Gabriella scowled over the comment but leaned closer to address me. "The last time you were here, Chauncey said you'd been weirded out by the portrait. I understand, Estella, if you're reluctant to go poking around."

I sighed and fiddled with the arrangement of gilded fall leaves around a votive candleholder that was on the table. "I suppose if I ducked out for a few minutes it would be a way to get folks to settle down. There's an awful lot of people gawking at me."

Cammy stood up. "That settles it."

"Fine, let's go." Resigned, I rose from my chair.

Drusilla and Gabriella rose as well and immediately started working the crowd to get their grand opening celebration back on track.

Philippe and Jacob crossed over to the bar—probably to smooth things over with the attendees—and I followed Cammy out of the ballroom.

We traveled down the hall, past the new reception area for the suites, and started up the staircase.

"There are four suites on the second floor," Cammy explained as we gained the second-floor landing. "And two even larger ones on the third."

We reached the top of the stairs, and I glanced over at my sister. "Which room did you find the amethysts in?"

Cammy threaded her arm through mine. "In what they're currently calling the Penthouse. It's the largest of all the suites. It has an attached living area, bedroom and a big spa-like bath. Come on, I'll show you." Cammy's phone sounded and she pulled it from her purse. "Damn it, Jacob wants me to come back downstairs and speak to someone about our wedding."

"Go ahead," I said, secretly relieved the ghost tour wouldn't be happening.

"Give me ten minutes," Cammy said. "While I'm gone you can check out the first suite." She pushed open a door and pointed.

"Go on." I waved her away. "Go find out what your fiancé wants."

She took off like a shot in towering heels and I stayed where I was, peering through the open doorway. Determined to kill some time, I walked farther down the hall. I'd managed about four steps before my stomach started to churn.

I'd never been up here before, but this section of the house seemed familiar to me. The hall took a turn and, intrigued, I followed it. The hallway was suddenly ice-cold. Like I'd stepped inside a walk-in freezer. Shocked, I stopped dead. A set of huge old windows were to my left and numbly, I recognized the large padded window seat tucked beneath them.

I'd seen this place before, I thought. *In my dreams.*

My mouth went bone dry as I vividly relived that dream I'd had about Pierre-Michel and Victoria making love. As I stood there, the lights began to flicker, and goose bumps raised on my arms. I shivered, imagining that I could almost hear their frantic whispers...

Je t'aime, Victoria...

I couldn't take my eyes off that window seat, and half-expected the couple to materialize right in front of me. When I saw my breath make puffs against the frigid air, I'd had enough. I swung back around, intending to make a run for it, and bounced right off of a man's chest.

I recoiled, even as he grabbed ahold of my arms to steady me, and I found myself face-to-face with Pierre-Michel. "My love," I heard myself say.

"Victoria, you've come back to me," he said. Then he swooped down, pulled me in close, and kissed the hell out of me.

For a couple of seconds a part of me rejoiced in being in his arms again. But when his whiskers rubbed across my face, my common sense caught up with my emotions.

Again? I wondered. *What Again? I'd never been in this man's arms before. He had stubble...and hadn't Pierre-Michel been clean shaven?*

The kiss went on, growing hotter, and while I was enjoying it immensely, another part of me was screaming that something wasn't right. *What was happening here?*

I yanked my mouth away, and saw for myself that it was Chauncey Marquette who'd been kissing me so passionately. "Chauncey?" I gave his arms a squeeze.

"Victoria?" He frowned down at me, and for a few seconds he looked as confused as I felt.

"Chauncey," I said, firmly. "It's me, Estella."

"Estella?" Chauncey frowned. "Is that you?" He shuddered, and I could tell the exact moment that he came completely back to himself. His eyes grew wide when he realized that he was holding me in his arms. "I beg your pardon." He sounded horrified as he released me and stepped back.

I shivered and took advantage of the window seat behind me. Slowly, I lowered myself to the cushion.

"Why is it so damn cold up here?" Chauncey demanded.

I saw movement out of the corner of my eye and let out a squeak as Pierre-Michel—or his ghost—was suddenly standing right beside Chauncey. Chauncey swore and jumped back in surprise.

"*Je t'aime, Victoria...*" the ghost said, reaching out for me.

I yanked away from Pierre-Michel's ghost so hard that my head bounced off the window frame. I felt the sharp pain, saw stars, and then...nothing.

***

When I opened my eyes, I realized two things. One: I was lying on a soft bed. And two: Someone was speaking to me and brushing the hair back from my face.

The gentleness was a novel experience for me and I sighed, turning my face toward that tender caress.

"There you are, sweetheart." The voice was low and husky.

Turning toward the voice, I slowly opened my eyes and discovered that a familiar man was sitting next to me on the bed. I jolted, and for a split second wondered if it was Pierre-Michel or Chauncey Marquette.

"Chauncey?" My voice came out in a squeak.

"In the flesh." He tipped his head to one side and smiled.

I breathed a sigh of relief, taking note of his contemporary dark suit, the modern-day hairstyle, and the man-scruff. "Is Pierre-Michel gone?"

"Yes," he said. "I think the ghost is gone, for now."

I started to sit up, and automatically felt for the back of my head. "Damn, my head hurts! What happened?"

He eased me back down. "You conked your head on the window frame and knocked yourself out."

I covered my eyes in mortification. "Well, fuck me!"

He burst out laughing. "Is that an offer?"

I yanked my hand away from my eyes "No! It sure the hell is *not*!" I sat bolt upright anyway, and the whole room went on a slow spin.

"Take it easy, I was only teasing." Chauncey chuckled, and patted my hand. "Why don't you sit back for a moment, Estella. You're still very pale."

I did as he suggested, and that sloshing feeling stopped. "I've never knocked myself out trying to get away from a ghost before," I said, crossing my arms over my chest. "I don't think I like it."

"Well, I didn't like it either." Chauncey patted my hand. "You scared me," he said. "When you went limp, the ghost vanished. So I picked you up and brought you in here."

"Where's in here?" I asked, looking around.

"Inside of one of the larger suites."

"Oh. It's nice. I guess." I took in the fancy area rug over gleaming hardwood floors, a stone fireplace, and the pretty gray and cream décor.

"Camilla showed up as I was carrying you. I told her what had happened and she said something about a level two phenomena, and took off to go get your sisters." He leaned forward, searching my face. "What do you remember?"

"I heard voices, the lights flickered and it got super cold," I said, as calmly as possible. "I was getting the hell out of there when I bounced off of you."

Chauncey sighed. "I heard the voices, felt the cold and then, *boom*."

"Right." I cleared my throat and met his eyes. "You said something about coming back to you, and then...you kissed me."

Chauncey didn't look away. "It was like stepping in someone else's life. I heard his voice inside my head, and his emotions became mine. He called you Victoria."

I nodded. "Yeah, you did—I mean *he* did."

Chauncey frowned. "Who the hell is Victoria? I thought Pierre-Michel's wife's name was Bridgette."

I cleared my throat. "I think that Victoria was his lover."

Chauncey's brows went up. "And you'd know that how?"

"Because this isn't the first time I've had contact with her. Ever since I moved here, I've had dreams, waking visions of the past, and the weirdest episodes of déjà vu. I think Victoria and Pierre-Michel saw an opportunity and jumped a ride on us—so to speak—so they could be together again."

"You are saying that a couple of ghosts *used* us so they could reenact their life?"

"A sort of possession thing, maybe. Cammy would be better able to explain what happened. She's the paranormal expert."

"I don't much care for the idea of possession."

"Well how else would you explain it, Marquette?" I smirked at him. "Or have you been harboring some secret passion, saw me in the hallway, and were so *overcome* that you just had to lay one on me?"

"Ah, *no*," Chauncey said, turning slightly red. "No offense."

"None taken," I said, and told myself to ignore the stupid disappointment I felt at his immediate denial.

"How are you feeling now?" he asked. "Think you can sit up?"

"I'm fine, Chauncey." I slowly sat up. "You don't have to hover."

He stayed exactly where he was, sitting beside me. For a few moments, he studied my face. "It's not a weakness to accept help from a friend, Estella."

Friends don't kiss each other like that. I almost said. Instead, I settled for, "I can more than take care of myself, Chauncey."

Chauncey nodded. "Yes, I saw tonight at the bar exactly how well you *can* handle yourself."

My eyebrows went up. "Is that a criticism?"

"No." He searched my eyes. "It was a compliment."

I felt butterflies in my stomach and it annoyed the hell out of me. Out of desperation, I tried for a joke. "Wow. You gave me a compliment. It's gone straight to my head."

"Head trauma." He said, straight faced. "Clearly it's addled your senses."

"Addled?" I laughed and rubbed the back of my head. "Who even talks like that anymore?"

Chauncey sat still, studying me like he'd never even seen me before. Suddenly uneasy, I licked my dry lips.

His reaction to the nervous gesture was to narrow his eyes. Carefully, he lifted a hand to my hair, and gently tucked a few wayward strands behind my ear.

That tender move had my heart leaping hard

in my chest. "Chauncey, I—"

"See?" he said, easing slightly closer. "It's not so hard letting a friend care for you."

Our eyes were now locked on each other and my heart sped up. His fingers slid behind my ear, cupping the side of my face, and then the door to the suite flew open, causing the two of us to jump apart.

"How's she doing?" Cammy strolled in, followed by Dru and Gabriella.

The spell broken, Chauncey stood and straightened his jacket. "She's awake and fine."

"Yeah," I said, watching as he brushed lint from his jacket sleeve. "I'm okay. No worries."

"I should return to help Philippe and Garrett with the event," Chauncey gave a nod to the group and slipped out of the room.

"Are you sure you're okay?" Gabriella sat next to me. "Your face is all red."

"Fine." I cleared my throat. "I would like to get the hell off of the third floor, though."

"I'll bet." Gabriella stood and held out a hand.

I swung my feet over the side of the bed and stood. When I didn't wobble, I started moving carefully toward the door.

When Dru snugged an arm around my waist as we went down the stairs, I didn't argue. I'd been embarrassed enough for one night. The last thing I wanted was to end up face planting again.

Drusilla and Gabriella went off to help their husbands and I settled in a table in the far corner of the lounge. I gratefully accepted the cup of tea that Cammy had brought over to me.

"We should talk," she said. "Let's start off with you telling me exactly what happened to you on the third floor."

"I'll try," I said, and quietly explained what I'd experienced upstairs.

"Spirit possession." Cammy let out a low whistle. "That's intense!"

"I'll say."

"Do you understand the term 'postcognition'?" Cammy asked.

I frowned. "Ah, no."

"Postcognition, or retro-cognition as it is sometimes called, is the psychic knowledge of the past," Cammy explained. "If that's your gift, it might explain why this has all been so intense for you."

I nodded. "Okay." I checked our surroundings, making sure no one was listening before I spoke. "Since I moved here I've been having these weird waking visions, like déjà vu. There's been some crazy intense dreams too. I'm starting to think that these visions and dreams might be memories from a long time ago." I gripped the mug tightly.

"I'm listening," Cammy said.

"It's like the memories, or scenes I see, are happening all out of order. I don't think I'm experiencing them in sequence. It's sort of hard to explain." I forced my fingers to loosen on the mug. "But it's like whatever they are, they're not my memories. It's more like they belong to someone else."

"Go on." Cammy gave my hand an encouraging pat.

"It's like I'm seeing another woman's life—through *her* eyes." I took a sip of the tea. "Some of the things I've seen were sweet. Some dreams were intense and scary, and some of it was...well let's say, intimate."

"Do you know what her name is?"

"Yes," I said. "I know her first name and the name of the man she loved."

Cammy seemed to hold her breath. "Who are, or *were* they?"

I blew out a careful breath. "After tonight, and what happened to Chauncey and me upstairs, I'm sure that they guy was Pierre-Michel Marquette."

"Whoa." Cammy's voice was low. "And the woman's name? Was it Bridgette?"

"His wife?" I shook my head. "No. In the dreams, and tonight he called me—I mean her —*Victoria*."

CHAPTER TEN

"So it's true," Cammy said, blowing out a long breath. "Victoria was in love with Pierre-Michel."

I did a double take. "Hang on a second. What do you know about this Victoria chick?"

Cammy reached out and took one of my hands. "She's our ancestor. Victoria Midnight was the one who wrote the prophecies about finding the Ames Dowry, and the lost star returning to Ames Crossing."

"Wait, you talked to me about that star prophecy before..." I narrowed my eyes. "But you failed to mention exactly *who* had written it."

Cammy shrugged. "At the time I didn't think it was important...obviously that was a big mistake on my part."

"Obviously," I said, sourly.

"Nevertheless, I should have followed up with you on that. I'm sorry."

I rubbed the back of my head and found a knot had formed. "So Victoria, Pierre-Michel's lover, was a daughter of Midnight? Holy shit."

Cammy blew out a long breath. "Holy shit, indeed."

"Well, why are her memories popping up in my dreams?" I hissed. "And why is she haunting me?"

Cammy rested her arms against the table. "I'm not sure. It does make me wonder if this is a past life memory situation for you. What if you are Victoria reincarnated?"

"That would mean Chauncey is..."

"Pierre-Michel," Cammy said. "Goddess knows he looks exactly like him."

"I wouldn't let Chauncey hear you say that. He hates that painting, and the shady history of his ancestor. Besides," I said firmly. "I don't believe in past lives."

"Well, I do," Cammy argued. "However, many things are different this time around."

I blinked. "Huh?"

"For starters, Chauncey isn't married, and you are *nothing* like Victoria."

"How the hell would you know that?" I asked.

"Because I've seen her portrait and I've read her journal." Cammy tapped a finger to her lips. "I'm more inclined to think you *are* a postcog—a psychic who senses the past."

"That information truly doesn't make me feel any better, Camilla."

"But it *does* explain why she wrote the prophecy about the lost star." My sister drummed her fingers on the tabletop as she thought it over. "Victoria knew you were coming and that someday in the future, you would help to tell her and Pierre-Michel's side of the story."

"You should be the one to explain all this to Chauncey," I said, leaning back in my chair. "He's even less happy about what happened to the two of us tonight than I am."

"I can hardly wait to discuss it with him." Cammy rubbed her hands together, clearly excited at the prospect. "Ghosts, and past lives?

This is going to be awesome."

I saw Chauncey across the room talking to some guests and wondered…*Would what happened between us tonight, change how he acted around me in the future? Or would he simply laugh it off as if it was no big deal?* I hadn't been looking in that direction, but now I had to admit that part of me was curious about Chauncey in a way I hadn't been before. *Damn you, Victoria...*

"This sucks," I said out loud.

Cammy gave my hand a squeeze. "Don't be embarrassed by what happened tonight, Estella. It's not like you had any control over the phenomenon. Neither of you did."

***

By the time the party ended a few hours later, I was more than ready to go back to the farmhouse. Once we'd arrived home Cammy handed over a slim, faded, hardback book.

"This is it?" I asked. The title on the cover said: *Love Poems*. "I thought you said you had her journal?"

“Look inside,” she urged. “She wrote all over the pages.”

I flipped through and saw a mish-mash of handwriting in all directions. Some of it was easy to read, while other sections were barely legible. “This is where you found the prophecies about the dowry and the lost star?”

“It is,” she said. “But take a look at the inscription on the first flagged page.”

I flipped open to the note marked ‘inscription’ and read. “*To my darling Victoria: forever yours, PM.*” I blew out a long breath. “One of the dreams I had was about them going on a picnic, where he gave her lilacs, and read poetry to her...I wonder if this was the same book?”

Cammy rested a hand on my shoulder. “I wouldn’t be surprised if it was. I think Victoria is showing you her memories for a reason.”

“I think you’re right.” I cleared my throat. “In one of the dreams I had of the two of them...they hooked up on that window seat in the mansion.”

“The one on the third floor where you and Chauncey kissed?”

"Bingo."

"No wonder you two had such a strong reaction to the environment." Cammy sat on the edge of the bed and patted the empty space next to her.

"Reaction to the environment. That's one way to put it." I sat beside her. "You're the ghost hunter. I'd have thought they'd have gone after you for their little reenactment." I waved the slim volume at her. "Why are the bastards picking on Chauncey and me?"

"For Chauncey, it's fairly obvious. He's a descendant and he resembles Pierre-Michel. But when it comes to you, Estella... I'm betting it's because of your psychic abilities."

"Look, Camilla, I didn't have any trouble like this with my *abilities,* as you call them, before I moved here."

"You only call me *Camilla* when you're pissed off. I just realized that." She pursed her lips. "I think the reason for the kick up in your abilities is because you didn't have much of an opportunity to put them to work before now. Besides, I think Victoria chose you because she figures you'd be the most sympathetic."

"How so?"

"Well you are the youngest of four siblings—like she was, and you know what it's like to be alone. To feel like you don't belong...anywhere."

I narrowed my eyes at her. "Stop doing that psychic shit on me. It's annoying as hell."

Cammy smiled. "But it's accurate, isn't it?"

I stood up. "I'm gonna read over this journal myself and see what I can find out."

My sister smiled. "All I ask is that the journal stays in the house. It's irreplaceable."

"Sure, no problem," I said.

Cammy pointed at the book. "The prophecy about the four stars of midnight is on a page I flagged with a pink sticky note."

"You tagged them?"

She nodded. "Yes. The most important passages. It's more organized and quicker to read that way. The spells are blue, the prophecies are pink, and her journal entries that made sense are marked in yellow notes. Random poetry I marked with green."

I looked more closely at the book and saw dozens of multicolored post-it notes marking individual pages. Each of them had a tiny note written across the top: Inscription, Ames/Midnight family prophecy, lost star prophecy, poetry, spells, charms...

"Jeez, Camilla, you really did color code it," I said. "Anal retentive much?"

Cammy wrinkled her nose. "Organization brings me joy."

I rolled my eyes. "Oh, for fucks sake."

"You're a Virgo as well, baby sister. Don't make fun of the personality traits of your own sun sign."

"I'm not into astrology," I said, heading for the door.

"That's all right." Cammy's voice was perky and cheerful. "I am."

I went to my room and stripped out of the pretty red dress. I hung it back on a hanger and pulled on an old t-shirt and my new flannel pajama bottoms. I plopped down in the middle of the bed and started reading. Mama Cat nosed open the door to my room and made herself at home next to me on the bed.

After an hour of studying the book, it became pretty obvious that Victoria had suffered from mental health issues. The earlier the entries, the more reasonable or clear they were...but after 1848, they all degraded into ramblings and nonsense.

I flipped back to the entry about me—the lost star—and took a picture of it with my cell phone. It was creepy the way her prophecy had been right on the money. I guessed she must have written it before she'd...I suppose the kindest thing to say was: before she'd become ill.

I closed my eyes for a moment against the sadness of it all. It didn't take a genius to figure out that after Pierre-Michel had died, Victoria had begun to slip into a serious depression, and then from the looks of it, madness.

So if I was supposed to be post-cog psychic, I thought. *What was I really supposed to know about Victoria and Pierre-Michel?* I sat up straight, kept my eyes closed, and took a deep breath. I counted my breaths and worked to be calm and centered.

"Okay, Victoria," I said after a moment. "Show me whatever it is I most need to know."

I opened my eyes, and the book at random.

Looking down, I focused on the first page I saw. Cammy had flagged it with a green post-it note. The penmanship was sloppy, and the entry date was listed as Summer 1848.

"Huh." I squinted at the handwriting. "It looks like a poem...sort of."

The longer I studied it, the more uncomfortable it made me. I tilted my head and carefully re-read the words. Telling myself there was absolutely no reason for my stomach to feel upset and for my shoulders to grow tight, yet they did anyway.

"What is this, exactly?" I mumbled to myself, and read it again.

Stolen away to be claimed by those who had none,
The most precious of gifts, shining bright like the sun.
I watch from afar, helpless, as the lie flourishes and grows,
While they live content in a house made of darkness and shadows.
This heritage of secrets will be passed down through the years,
Generations of evil that no one should have to

bear.
When the Spring equinox moon turns to ash, all wrongs will be made right,
Revealed by a shining star, and a secret daughter of Midnight.

The cool October breeze from my open bedroom window made goose bumps rise on my arms. "This *is* sort of spooky." I shivered. "And damn it, I hope that 'star' part of her poem isn't another reference to me."

Going on impulse, I snapped a picture of the weird entry marked "Random Poetry," by Cammy, and decided to call it a night. I was too tired to think straight anymore, so I got up, pulled the covers back and dove under them. I plugged in my phone to charge and placed the book on the nightstand.

While the cat made herself at home and snuggled up next to me, I clicked off the lamp on the bedside table. With a huge yawn, I pulled the quilt up to my chin and dropped off into sleep.

***

The next morning I had the day off, and I decided to check out the local library and see if I could dig up any more history on the town, and Pierre-Michel's big scandal of 1847. What happened at the mansion last night had changed things for me. I felt a push to search for answers and I never ignored my gut when I felt like this. So research mode: on.

I thought it best to stay clear of the old haunted house for a while. Sure, I could have gone to the mansion and hit the museum room Gabriella had set up, but I wanted to take a look through the history of the town on my own—with no ghosts horning in.

Note to self, I thought. *Stop at Lotions & Potions and stock up on lilac scented soap and perfume. Cammy had said lilacs were good for banishing ghosts...*

I still had Amanda Beaumont's card, and I intended to pay her a visit to see if she could give me a hand. Librarians got paid to help people research, right? Anyway, she seemed like my most logical choice for information. Neutral information.

I loaded up my bag with change for the copy

machine and added a legal pad from Cammy's stash of office supplies. It was chilly today, so I wore my new orange sweater and my favorite jeans. I tugged on my ankle boots, shrugged on my denim jacket and was out the door by 9am.

The town's small library was a block down from *Camilla's Lotions & Potions*. I entered the library a bit after opening and headed straight for the front desk. Before I even reached it, Amanda came out from a back office. I waved at her and she smiled.

I was suddenly glad I'd taken the time to bust out all the cosmetics this morning. Since Amanda was dressed in a style I guess could best be described as *Librarian chic*. Her hair tumbled down her back in loose curls, and her glasses were different today. Instead of the blush frames, these were a more cat-eye shaped and a dusty purple.

She walked over wearing a tweed pencil skirt and a dark blue cardigan over a sheer blouse. The shoes were gray-blue and laced up with a wide ribbon. With thick chunky heels and a pointy toe, they managed to be both classy and sexy.

Self consciously, I adjusted the simple headband I'd added to my own hair. Gabriella had left the headband behind at the farmhouse, so I'd borrowed it. I told myself not to be intimidated by Amanda's style. But I was anyway.

I smiled and stuck out my hand. "Hi Amanda. I was wondering if you had a few minutes?"

She shook my offered hand. "Of course! What can I do for you today?"

"I was hoping you could help me with some local history. From the mid 1800's."

"Follow me to the local history section," she said.

With a nod, she led the way and stopped in front of the shelves. She glanced back and as she did, sunlight poured in from a window above. Her hair, which I'd taken as brown, seemed to light up with different shades of copper.

That explained the freckles, I thought.

She narrowed one eye as I stared. "Are you researching the missing bride?"

"In a way." Self-consciously I slid the blue

goldstone star pendant on its chain. "It's sort of complicated."

Amanda checked our immediate surroundings and tugged me deeper in the stacks. "Tell me."

"I'm trying to find out more about Pierre-Michel Marquette and a woman he was romantically involved with."

"Did you learn about the scandal of 1847 from your friend, Camilla?"

"She's not my friend," I said, bluntly.

"Oh?" Amanda blinked. "You're working with her at *Lotions & Potions,* aren't you?"

Now it was my turn to blink. "How'd you know that?"

"Small towns," Amanda explained in a low, library voice. "Plus, I've seen you working in the shop."

Gossip spread like wildfire in small towns...and word about me would get out soon enough, I thought. *Besides, I'd be more comfortable if it happened on my terms.* "Honestly, Camilla Midnight isn't just my boss," I said, softly. "She's my sister."

Amanda's eyes grew round. "I thought your

last name was Flores."

"Technically my middle name is Flores—I went by that when I lived in California. My legal surname is Midnight."

Amanda went very still. "You are a daughter of Midnight?"

Her words caused me to feel a hitch between my shoulder blades. "Me, Dru, Gabriella and Cammy, all shared the same father—Daniel—so I suppose that's one way of putting it."

Her eyes narrowed as she considered me. "So, are you researching your family tree?"

"In a round about way." I hesitated for a moment and then went with my gut. "Well, the thing is...I have reason to believe that Victoria Midnight was involved with Pierre-Michel Marquette back in 1847."

Amanda's eyebrows went way up. "Why do you believe that?"

There was something about Amanda. Instinctively, I knew I could trust this woman. I blew out a long breath and took the leap of faith. "Because since I moved here I've had visions and dreams about Pierre-Michel and a woman he called Victoria. Basically, I've been seeing the past through her eyes."

I gave her the short version of what I'd come to know, what had happened at the mansion last night, and Camilla's paranormal theories.

When I finished, she blew out a long breath. "Fascinating," Amanda murmured. "So what you're experiencing are random vignettes from the past, and not in any particular sequence?"

I shrugged. "I don't know for sure, but my gut says, it's all out of order." I stopped and checked to make sure no one was close enough to eavesdrop. There'd been more than a few older ladies hovering since I'd arrived.

Amanda glanced around. "It's all clear," she said.

I nodded. "In fact, I think that the first dream—the one of them on the cliffs—may have been to show me what happened between them *after* his wife disappeared. He was desperate to have her run away with him and I—I mean *Victoria*, she ran from him. She was terrified."

"Between that and the incident last night, I can see why you'd want some answers," Amanda said.

"Anyway," I said, "I wondered if I could find

any actual historical *proof* that they'd been, you know, a couple."

Amanda leaned slightly forward, studying my face. "You know, the longer I look at you the more I see a resemblance to Gabriella."

I pointed to my dark hair. "Yeah, I'm often mistaken for blue-eyed blondes. Happens every day."

Amanda grinned. "No, I meant the shape of your face, your features...Coloring aside, you strongly resemble Gabriella. More so than Dru, or even Camilla does."

I shrugged, and repeated what Gabriella had once said to me. "Genetics are a funny thing."

"There's no escaping from that, is there?" Her eyes suddenly intense, Amanda stopped smiling.

I hesitated before responding, because I had the weirdest feeling that we were no longer talking about the same thing. I sensed that she was being honest with me, but there was something else. *Something that she didn't want me to know. Or was worried about me finding out...*I cleared my throat. "Anyway..." I tried a smile. "About that local history?"

Amanda seemed to shake herself back to the present. "Come with me," she said. "I'll set you up with some books and recent articles concerning the local history."

I spent a pleasant few hours reading and discovered since Cammy and Jacob had found the missing dowry last year, that there had been a resurgence of articles both about the history of the Ames family *and* the Marquettes.

Everything Cammy had told me pretty much matched up to the articles I read. Bridgette and Pierre-Michel, the whole arranged marriage thing. How his bride had disappeared in the summer of 1847. Neither her dowry or her body had been found, yadda, yadda, yadda. I found it very interesting that while Pierre-Michel had been *suspected* of murdering his bride, he'd never formally been accused. Then Pierre-Michel had died later that same year.

It made me shake my head over the waste of so many lives. First Bridgette went missing, next Pierre-Michel had died in an accident, and finally Victoria had slowly gone mad. The Ames, Marquette, *and* the Midnight families all had been affected by the scandal in one form or another.

As of last year, the family had set things to right...for the most part. The amethyst jewelry had been found and returned to the Ames. According to Cammy, even though they hadn't found her remains, Bridgette's spirit was now at rest...

But what about Pierre-Michel and Victoria?

I rested my chin on my hand and thought it over. Considering everything I'd been experiencing, those two souls certainly weren't at peace. I guessed the term 'star-crossed lovers' applied. Thinking back on the dreams I'd had, they'd been crazy in love with each other. Not to mention that the passion I'd felt from Chauncey—scratch that—Pierre-Michel, had been on an epic scale.

What had it done to Victoria's state of mind to have her lover taken away from her not once…but twice?

I decided to write down everything I could remember from the dreams and the visions I'd had since coming to Ames Crossing. I filled up several pages in the legal pad, and tried to figure what chronological order they went in.

I'd bet the whole dance thing, the déjà vu episode that I'd had while dancing with Chauncey, had happened early on in their relationship. Maybe the flashback in the hall was next...The romantic picnic seemed like a logical step. Then the window seat hook-up, and finally the dream of them on the cliffs where Victoria had run away from him in fear...

Lost in my thoughts, I was casually scanning the reprints of the old newspaper articles from 1847 when I saw the quote from Mary Ames, Bridgette's sister. She'd gone on record as saying that "justice had finally been served," at the announcement of Pierre-Michel's death.

So how did he die? I wondered, trying to remember if anyone had actually told me. Determinedly, I flipped back through the articles trying to find out. It made me go cold to discover that he'd died in a carriage accident on the 31st of October. "Holy shit," I whispered. "He died on Halloween night?"

"Estella?" Amanda's soft voice had me jumping a foot straight up in the air.

I patted my heart back in place. "Yeah?"

"My afternoon meeting is a no-show, and so

I have the rest of the day off. I was wondering if you'd like to get lunch?"

There was something I liked about the librarian, and I had a strong hunch that we could become friends with very little effort. "Lunch sounds great." I smiled.

She smiled in return. "Well, what do you say we put all your research materials away and blow this popsicle stand. I have some information at my home that might be helpful."

"Really?" I started to stack my notes and papers.

"Yes." She nodded. "That way we can talk privately about your ancestor and the scandal of 1847 without folks trying to eavesdrop."

"Perfect," I said.

CHAPTER ELEVEN

I followed Amanda to her house for lunch. It was only a few blocks away from the main street, and the two-story was nestled between the road and the base of smaller cliffs. The house was tidy with white trim that managed to accent its funky lines. There were small additions jutting off the sides of the home, making the shape of the house more interesting.

The foundation of the house was made with the same limestone I'd seen in other historic homes in the village, but the upper two thirds had been covered in more modern pale gray siding. Narrow steps made of the same limestone went up to a black front door and tiny covered porch. I could see some orange lights around the door, and a pumpkin sat on the topmost step.

I exited my car and followed her around to the side of the home. Her side yard was sunny and large with flowerbeds scattered around. Toward the back of the property was a small flat area that ended with a thin strip of woods. Where the trees stopped, the base of the cliffs began.

I followed her up wooden steps. We crossed a nice sized deck and went in a side door of the house.

"Come in, and welcome," she said, and to my surprise, opened the apparently unlocked door and walked in.

"You don't lock your house?" I asked.

Amanda smirked, and held the door for me. "Trust me. No one can break in here."

"Fancy security system?" I asked, following her in to a kitchen with sage green cabinets.

"Something like that." She set her purse down on the kitchen table. "Take a seat," she said, and went directly to the refrigerator.

"I like your kitchen, Amanda," I said, looking around at the ivory painted bead board walls, wood floor and sturdy old farmhouse table. “It’s cozy.” No sooner had I spoken when the overhead light in the kitchen appeared to grow brighter.

Amanda smiled up at the light fixture. “It seems to like you, as well.”

“How’s that?” I asked.

“Some houses have a spirit, you might say.”

“We talking about a ghost or more of a personality?”

Amanda nodded her head. “Personality, in this case. The Beaumont house is old and has held onto many memories.”

“How very Dracula-esque.” I raised my eyebrows at her.

Amanda pressed a hand to her heart. “You caught the play on a literary quote. We can definitely be friends.”

“Hey, I may not have gone to college, but I’ve been known to read a book or two.”

“I’m happy to hear that,” she said, straight faced. “We should see about getting you a library card, immediately. All the cool kids have one.”

I couldn’t help but laugh. “You’re a smart-ass, Amanda.”

"Guilty." Amanda gestured to a wooden chair painted in the same vintage green of the cabinets, and I took a seat as she went to the fridge. "How do you feel about herbed chicken salad?"

I smiled. "Sounds good to me."

While she puttered around making sandwiches, I admired the homey kitchen. A few small pumpkins were placed on the countertops, and there was a huge decorated Halloween wreath hanging on the inside of the back door. I was about to comment on the holiday decorations when a scruffy black cat strolled in. Its tail held high, the cat jumped directly on top of the kitchen table.

"Hi kitty." I held out my hand and the cat leaned in, allowing me to rub its ears.

"That's Nyx," Amanda said.

"Like the Greek goddess of the night?"

"Exactly." Amanda turned around and grinned. "You want chips or carrot sticks with your sandwich?"

"Chips," I said, and noted the herbs drying from beams overhead.

Of course there were books on shelves—I'd

have expected no less from a librarian. There were also pretty colored glass jars on the counter and a large stained-glass panel in deep jewel tones hanging over the kitchen sink window. The panel featured an upright five-pointed star. My lips twitched as I spotted a rustic sign that hung on the soffit above her cabinets. It was a distressed white and read, *There's A Little Witch In All Of Us.*

Between the herbs, stained-glass pentagram, the overall vibe of her home, *and* the name of her cat, I figured she was most likely a practitioner.

I watched as my new friend bustled around her kitchen. She didn't fit the type of witches I'd known in California. In public, Amanda blended in with everyone else. Most witches I'd known were more flamboyant or edgy, like Cammy. Amanda's discreet academic vibe really contrasted with her classically witchy house, and it made me curious. "Are you into witchcraft, Amanda?"

"I am," she answered easily. "However I tend to keep a fairly low profile." She pulled two cans of soda from the fridge and slid them across the table.

"With your job as a librarian, I get that." I picked up my soda and popped the top. "Seems like most practitioners do the same around here...except maybe for Cammy."

Amanda smiled and continued to make the sandwiches. "You've been living in Ames Crossing for a while now. Surely you've figured out that this area is filled with witches, magick, and ghosts."

"Can't argue that, especially after my experience yesterday." I scratched the cat under its chin. "Why do you suppose that is?"

"My theory is that it has something to do with the fact that the two largest rivers on the continent meet here."

I ripped open the bag of chips and helped myself. "So, are we talking, like, ley lines?"

"Yes." Amanda nodded. "Both paranormal phenomenon *and* magick users are often attracted to places where ley lines intersect."

I nodded. "Sure, I've heard that theory before."

She walked over and set a plate in front of me. "Would it surprise you to find out that there are other haunted houses in the village, beside the Marquette mansion?"

"Nope, I wouldn't be surprised..." I trailed off, studying her as she took a seat beside me.

Nyx gave a loud and long *meow* and swatted at Amanda's arm.

Amanda seemed to nod to the cat. "I told you at the library that I had some information that might be helpful..."

"Yes?"

"Well, since you trusted me enough to share your experiences about Pierre-Michel and Victoria Midnight; I'll return the favor and tell you about my own connection to the scandal of 1847."

"Connection?" I picked up my sandwich. "What connection?" I asked.

"How much has your grandmother filled you in on the Midnight family tree?"

"A little bit." I took a bite of my sandwich.

Amanda sampled a chip. "Would you mind if I asked exactly how much?"

I rested my elbows on the table. "She told me about her husband, and that she raised my sisters after their mother dumped them and took off."

"Anything farther back?" Amanda asked. "Anything about your ancestors?"

I shook my head. "No. She didn't."

"I see." Amanda blew out a long breath.

Amanda was testing the waters, I realized. *She was wondering how I would react to whatever she was about to say.* "What are you trying to tell me, Amanda?"

"The thing is," she said, "I don't think we met by accident last night. I think, maybe, it was fate."

I tipped my head over to one side. "How so?"

She tucked a long copper curl behind her ear. "Are you aware that Victoria Midnight was one of four Midnight siblings?"

"Yes, Cammy talked about that literally the other day. There was one boy and three girls," I said, thinking it over. "It was the son, who me and my sisters are descended from—according to her."

"That would have been Tobias Midnight," she said. "He did indeed have three sisters: Jenna, Louisa and Victoria." Amanda looked me directly in the eye. "Has anyone in your family ever mentioned what happened to the other two daughters of Midnight?"

"No, they didn't." I set my sandwich back on the plate. "But I'm gonna take a wild guess that you are about to. So, what do you know about the rest of the Midnight family?"

Amanda gathered the cat in her arms as she spoke. "Tobias and his descendants stayed on the family farm."

"The same place where my grandmother lives now?"

"The one and the same." Amanda confirmed as the cat began to purr, loudly.

"Okay," I said. "I knew the place was old. What about the rest of them?"

"Jenna Midnight married a merchant and moved to St. Louis," Amanda explained. "Which left Louisa and Victoria. Louisa and her husband settled here in Ames Crossing. They had only one child, Victor."

"Named after her sister, Victoria?" I guessed.

"That's what we figure." Amanda nodded. "Victoria never married, and after the scandal she went to live with her sister Louisa. For a few years anyway...eventually she became too ill and had to be institutionalized."

"Institutionalized?" A chill rolled down my back. "That's awful."

"Yes, it is," Amanda agreed.

"And you know all this stuff because you're really into the history of the village?"

"I know all this," she said, "because the son of Louisa Midnight and Eugene Beaumont, was Victor James Beaumont. Victor, was my great-great-great grandfather."

I did a double take. "Louisa Midnight is *your* ancestor?"

"Yes," she said, and the back door suddenly blew open and bounced off the kitchen wall.

"*Shit*!" I couldn't help but jump at the loud noise.

Amanda, I noticed, didn't so much as blink. She sat there cool as a cucumber, holding her cat and waiting for my reaction to the family news.

I studied her carefully. "That would make you a daughter of Midnight as well."

"That's right," Amanda said. "You and I are actually fourth cousins."

"No wonder you were so surprised when I

told you Cammy was my sister." Shocked at her revelation, I scrubbed a hand over my face. "How come Priscilla and my sisters never told me about having other relatives in town?"

"Because they don't know."

I narrowed my eyes. "Why are you keeping that a secret?"

"According to what my grandfather told me, the Beaumont's have purposefully hidden their links to the Midnight family. They've done so for decades."

"Why?" I asked again.

"Because not all the Midnight's practiced positive magick." Amanda sighed. "Louisa Midnight, my four times great grandmother, was dark. She was hired to work a death-curse on Pierre-Michel Marquette, and she was happy to take the job."

It took me a moment. I had to let the information sink in. "So who hired Louisa?"

"Mary Ames," Amanda said. "My grandfather told us, that *his* grandfather told him that she was paid, very, very well to work the curse."

"Bridgette's sister paid Louisa to put the

whammy on Pierre-Michel?" I sat back in my chair and thought about the old newspaper quote where Mary said that 'justice had finally been served'.

"The Ames family was influential in those days, and extremely wealthy," Amanda said. "Mary Ames could afford to buy whatever she wanted."

I raised my eyebrows. "Except that all the money in the world couldn't bring her sister back."

"Very true." Amanda nodded in agreement. "According to her journals, Louisa cast the curse on Samhain eve, and the magick hit home within hours...

"*Shit*," I whispered in awe. "Because Pierre-Michel died on October thirty-first, Halloween night."

"Which explains why his spirit never found rest," Amanda said. "Being accused of murder, and ultimately dying at the hands of a pissed-off witch pretty much ensures that a soul is doomed to wander."

"Ghosts often hang around because of unfinished business," I said. "That's like ghost hunting 101."

"Exactly." Amanda nodded. "But it seems that Louisa wasn't merely satisfied with causing his death...because the Marquette family had nothing but the worst of luck with their land here in Illinois, for generations."

I thought back to everything Gabriella had told me about the old vineyard and how prohibition had wiped it out in the 1920's. Then a new thought hit me, and I gasped. "How long ago was it that Philippe, Garrett Rivers, and Brooke's father started rejuvenating the Marquette family property, with plans to open a winery and someday the mansion for business?"

"Only a few years ago." Amanda's voice was serious and sad.

"Oh my god. Brooke," I whispered.

"The Marquettes had abandoned the mansion for almost a century before Philippe and his friends Garrett and Barry came back, invested, and began to renovate the vineyards and the family manor," Amanda said. "Sadly, Brooke's parents have been the most recent tragedy involving the Marquette property."

"Are you saying that her parents' death wasn't a random accident? Do you think that it was related to the curse?"

"I don't know for certain," Amanda said, "but what I do know is *after* the modern-day daughters of Midnight began to become involved with the remaining partners, things began to change. First Drusilla and Garrett fell in love, and the winery opened without incident. Drusilla and Garrett have thankfully made things so much better for that poor girl."

"Agreed," I said.

Amanda adjusted her glasses. "To continue, Gabriella and Philippe met, but were pulled apart for a time because of Chauncey's racing accident."

My stomach dropped to my shoes. "Chauncey might have suffered from the curse too?"

"I'd say it's a strong possibility. But think about the big picture. Gabriella and Philippe reunited, fell in love, began to build their family and eventually married."

I started to connect the dots. "And so with another daughter of Midnight in the picture, the

Marquettes' luck seemed to improve again. When Cammy and Jacob Ames became involved, they ended up finding Bridgette's missing dowry inside the mansion," I said.

Amanda smiled. "Once again a daughter of Midnight changed the circumstances for the better."

I considered Amanda as she sat there, quiet, and pretty with her copper hair tumbling over her back. "You've been watching over them all this whole time, haven't you?"

Amanda blushed. "Yes, and I've tried to help them from behind the scenes, whenever or however I could."

"I think you should tell my grandmother who you really are," I said. "You have nothing to be ashamed of. It's not your fault who your ancestor was. Nor are you responsible for what that old witch did for revenge, back in the day."

"Louisa paid for what she'd unleashed on Pierre-Michel," Amanda said. "The price of the curse she cast was high, and it slowly but surely took away what Louisa held most dear."

"How so?" I asked.

"As the curse rebounded, she worked more

and more magick in an effort to nullify it, or at least gain some semblance of control over it... But her husband, Eugene, died within a year, leaving her a widow with a young child." Amanda shook her head. "Still, Louisa kept practicing and working. From what we know, folks came to her for hexes and curses for years."

A chill rolled down my back at the thought. "So the dark arts paid well, did it?"

"She managed to keep her house, live comfortably, and send her son away to college. Unfortunately, after all the years of dark magick, it contaminated her house and the land it stands on."

I studied the kitchen with new eyes. "Which left her son and his descendants to do the clean-up."

"Sadly, yes." Amanda said. "Louisa left behind a dark heritage that both my grandfather and father did their best to keep locked down, and under control. Think of Louisa's magick like a toxin. One that is long lasting, influencing the environment for generations."

"I get that you feel you have a duty," I

argued. "But you and your family shouldn't have to pay for someone else's mistakes."

Amanda sighed. "I was always taught that it was my responsibility to make sure that the echoes of whatever Louisa did here on this land, stays contained. When I came of age, I took over the burden from my father."

"So basically, you and your family are magickal guardians?"

Amanda nodded. "Essentially, yes. I've spent a lifetime studying and preparing to be the caretaker of the property, like my father and grandfather and great-grandfather before me. Over the decades we've worked to reverse whatever evil is here, and we've had some luck getting the house to cooperate."

I did a double take. "You have had luck getting the *house* to cooperate?"

"This was *her* house, Estella. It's got a will of its own."

I narrowed my eyes. "Meaning what, exactly?"

"I suppose the best way to explain is simply to show you," Amanda said. She set the cat on the floor and raised one hand. "Shut down," she said, and instantly the back door slammed shut, and the locks flipped.

On their own.

"Friend," she said next, and the lights became brighter. The house was suddenly warmer and felt more inviting.

"You can get a voice assistant like *Alexa*, to turn up the lights and heat these days..." I started to say, and then fell silent when the windows began to raise, allowing the breeze to come in.

"This isn't what you'd call a 'smart house,' Estella," Amanda said.

I did my best to get words to form. "Oh," was about all I could manage. *This wasn't a joke. She was totally telling the truth.*

"Foe," Amanda said next, and the windows banged shut. The cat went bolting from the room with a screech, and the kitchen became darker and noticeably colder...but more alarming than that, was the *feeling* it invoked.

I swallowed hard, and felt goose bumps break out on my arms. My chest grew tight and my heart began to race. I wanted out of her house, badly. The compulsion to run was so real that I strained against it.

Amanda dropped a hand on my shoulder. “Do you understand, now?”

“I believe you,” I said. “Can we turn off the show?”

“Desist!” Amanda said firmly, and instantly the lights were brighter, the room was more comfortable, I started to relax, and it felt easier to breathe.

“Holy shit,” I said, as the windows slid back up and the cat crept back in the room. Nyx ran to her Mistress for comfort, and Amanda bent and picked the cat up.

“Now you see why I can’t reveal myself to the other Midnights,” Amanda said. “Not when my heritage is *this*.”

“I don’t agree, but, I’ll keep the secret for now.” I pushed the other kitchen chair out with my foot. “In the meantime, why don’t you sit down and we can eat our lunch.”

“I half-expected you to run screaming from the house.” Amanda chuckled and sat. Nyx jumped down and sat between our chairs, flipping her tail.

“Ha! I got possessed by a lovesick ghost last

night. You don't scare me, *chica*." The back door opened slightly. "Your house doesn't scare me either," I said loudly, and the door opened the rest of the way, and the air seemed to sigh.

Amanda grinned. "You're a ballsy, yet practical woman. I like that about you."

"I still think you should tell my grandmother and sisters about your links to the Midnight family." I took a bite of my chicken salad. "When the time is right."

"I will, someday," Amanda said, and jumped to her feet. "You know what? This calls for a drink." She went to her fridge, pulled out a bottle of wine and snagged two glasses from the cabinet.

"I won't argue with that," I said as she sat back down at the table and poured two glasses of wine from the *Trois Ames* winery.

"To new friends," Amanda said and raised her wineglass.

I tapped my glass to hers. "And to relatives. I sure do have a hell of a lot more of them than I ever imagined."

"After we finish lunch," Amanda said, "why don't we start working on figuring out why

Pierre-Michel and Victoria's ghosts are so intent on reaching out to you and Chauncey."

"Cammy thinks it's a past life thing, but knowing what I do now, I don't agree."

"Hmm." Amanda took another sip of wine. "You know, I bet I have some spells that can keep them from taking possession of you and Chauncey again. That is, if you're interested, cousin."

"That'd be *great*," I said. "Because my gut tells me that the ghosts aren't finished with us yet."

"I don't think they are either," she said. "But I bet between the two of us we can figure out a way to keep them out of your head, and maybe even put an end to Louisa's curse once and for all."

I sat in that bewitched kitchen, and for the first time in a long while—felt as if I belonged. Like I was a part of something. I had family, a new friend, *and* I had an almost two-hundred-year-old mystery to solve.

I lifted my glass. "I may not officially be a wise woman yet, however between Cammy and you showing me the ropes...It's only a matter of time."

"To the daughters of Midnight," Amanda said, raising her glass to mine.

"Let's kick some ass," I said, and tapped my glass against hers.

Turn the page for a sneak peek of book 5 in the "Daughters Of Midnight" Series.

Midnight Secrets

Prologue

No one ever expects that a small-town librarian would have a secret life. If you glanced at me while I was at work, most likely all you would see is a thirty-year-old, red-haired woman quietly sitting at the reference desk.

Which is exactly what I would *want* you to see.

Not drawing attention to myself does, in fact, make what I do much easier. Blending in and flying under the radar was an essential part of my life, and an asset to my calling. Now when I say, 'calling,' I'm not speaking of my day job as the branch manager of the Ames Crossing public library. No indeed.

This is about my *other* job.

A teenage girl approached the reference desk, and I met her eyes and smiled. "May I help you?"

"Hello, Ms. Beaumont. I was wondering—" Her voice broke and she nervously cleared her throat. "Do you have any books on ghosts?"

I smiled. Ghosts and hauntings are a very popular topic locally. "Yes, we do." I stood and smoothed down my dark blue pencil skirt. "Follow me, please."

I walked her over to the non-fiction section, then turned down the rows. I didn't bother glancing over my shoulder to see if she was following. Nervous energy was spiking off her and felt like sharp prickles brushing against my back. I paused and indicated a few books to the teen. "These two titles would be good for you to start with. They have basic information about the different types of hauntings."

"Do any of those books tell you how to get rid of a ghost?" she asked.

I nodded. "A few."

"Thank you," she said, and pulled one of the books I'd shown her.

I resisted the urge to pat her on top of her head, and instead pointed out a table where she could read and left her to it.

I made my way back to the front, stopping to

pick up a discarded children's book from the middle of the floor. It hadn't been there a moment ago. Turning my head, I saw a young mother frantically trying to keep up with her toddler who was running amok in the children's section. 'Timothy the Terror' was loose in the library once again.

"Timothy!" His mother's mortified whisper cut through the calm of the library.

Timothy was not quite three years old, and he was tossing books left and right as he worked his way down the stacks. I stopped at the end of the row, folded my arms and waited for him. The toddler was still running full out when he smacked into my legs, rebounded, and then ended up on his butt. His rampage had come to a screeching halt.

The book he was carrying bounced off the floor and landed on the pointy toes of my long black boots. "Hello, Timothy." I gave him my firmest librarian's scowl.

"Uh-oh." His eyes were huge as he stared up at me.

"We do not throw books in the library," I said. "Nor do we run, or act rowdy."

His bottom lip began to tremble.

"Now," I said. "I want you to go back and pick up all the books you knocked to the floor and bring them to me. Quietly."

"Okay." With tears in his eyes, he nodded and turned around to do so.

"I'm sorry," Timothy's mother said. She was heavily pregnant and carrying several fallen books. "He just got a little over excited."

I took the books from her arms. "Looks like you have your hands full."

She blew her bangs out of her eyes. "So much for me thinking I could pick up a few romances to read."

"We have a display by the check-out counter of newer release romance novels. Why don't you leave Timothy to me, and go pick out a few books for yourself?"

"You'd do that for me?"

"Of course." I smiled and sent her along. When I turned back to check on Timothy, he had picked up most of the books and placed them into a neat stack on the carpet.

"I picked the books all up," he said, gravely.

I nodded. "What a good job you've done." I

notice the dinosaur on his sweatshirt and pulled a large picture book off the top shelf. "Here is a book on dinosaurs that I think you'll like."

Timothy accepted the book with a smile. "I like pictures!"

While Timothy grinned over the illustrations, I selected a few more popular picture books and held out my hand to him. "Let's take these up to the check-out counter and you can take them home to read."

"Okay!" Timothy tucked the book under one arm, grabbed my hand, and happily followed me to the front.

After they had checked out, I waved goodbye to the little hellion and his beleaguered mother. *Peace once again reigned in my library, and I hadn't even had to break out any magick,* I thought. *If only all problems with monsters were so easily solved.*

My name is Amanda Beaumont. I live in Ames Crossing, Illinois, where the two largest rivers in North America meet. In this location we have an intersection of several ley lines. These natural conduits of energy attract paranormal phenomena of all types, such as:

cryptids, monsters, ghosts, and last but not least, witches.

Because of the latter, I'm bound to an inheritance I never asked for. For my family line has been tasked with keeping the balance between good and evil. While modern-day practitioners such as the Midnight family are locally known for their gentle wise-women practices, and herbalism...not all the members of their family were goodness and light.

Several generations ago, one individual in the Midnight family was quite dark. She was notorious for working hexes and curses, and her avocation paid quite well. Her name was Louisa Midnight. How can I be so sure of what Louisa did? Because, Louisa Midnight married Eugene Beaumont. They had only one son, Victor, who was born in 1848.

Victor Beaumont was my three times great-grandfather, which meant that *I* was a direct descendant of Louisa Midnight.

Yes, I too am a daughter of Midnight, albeit a secret one.

Over the years, the Beaumont branch of the Midnight family tree was forgotten—and the

Beaumonts worked hard to make that happen. My great-grandfather, grandfather, and father have each worked behind the scenes trying to restore the balance and to minimize the damage that Louisa's curses have wrought.

The Beaumonts have become the keepers of a chilling heritage—Louisa's home, property, her personal papers, journals, and spell books. My predecessors have done their best to clean up the energetic chaos that Louisa had left in her wake...And now it's my turn. Today, I am the most recent Guardian of Ames Crossing.

Hence that *other* job I mentioned.

I had been studying, preparing and working my whole life to take over this task from my father. But instead of watching from afar, for the first time in generations, a Beaumont had made contact with our distant relatives, the Midnights.

When the invitation to attend the grand opening of the hotel suites at the Marquette Mansion had dropped in my lap, I'd taken it. I simply swallowed my distaste for the odious man who'd invited me, and went. It was the perfect opportunity to get an up-close look at the mansion, and to learn more about the family that had started all the drama two hundred years ago. It also had granted me the chance to rub elbows *anonymously* with my distant cousins, the Midnights, at the same time.

Unfortunately, the evening hadn't gone quite as I'd envisioned it...

In my mind I would have been much more graceful, poised and powerful. Getting manhandled, and then knocked on my backside by an over-amorous drunk, hadn't been one of the scenarios I'd envisioned. But I should know better than anyone, that fate often has its own plans.

In the end, it was Estella Flores who had come to my aid. She then surprised me further by seeking me out later for information *and* revealing that she was part of the Midnight family.

The incident Estella was interested in involved an almost two-hundred-year-old murder mystery. A mystery that still had folks in the village talking about it, and an unsolved crime the Beaumont family—my family—believes was made even worse by Louisa and her dark magick.

I hadn't expected to like her, but Estella was *nothing* like the rest of the current-day Midnight family. She was a feisty Latina, strong, tough and streetwise. That sheen of faery tale enchantment that had blessed her trio of half-sisters hadn't rubbed off on Estella.

Nor had it rubbed off on me.

I tucked a strand of my auburn hair back into the bun I'd worn today. *Apparently the faery tale only applied to the blondes in the family…* I smirked to myself.

The rest of us had to work when it came to magick.

***

Midnight Secrets
Daughters of Midnight, Book 5
Coming Soon

ABOUT THE AUTHOR

Ellen Dugan is the award-winning author of over twenty-eight books. Ellen's popular non-fiction titles have been translated into over twelve foreign languages. She branched out successfully into paranormal fiction with her popular *Legacy Of Magick, The Gypsy Chronicles,* and *Daughters Of Midnight* series. Ellen has been featured in USA TODAY'S HEA column. She lives an enchanted life in Missouri tending to her extensive perennial gardens and writing. Please visit her website and blog:

www.ellendugan.com
www.ellendugan.blogspot.com

Made in the USA
Middletown, DE
13 June 2019